C000156120

Dream Within

Pirate Gold

Ah Wesson

So many thank yous

are due to you

"

love
Alex ✦

Alexander Randall 5th

Copyright © 2022 by Alexander Randall 5th.

All rights reserved. No part of this publication may be reproduced, distributed, or transmitted in any form or by any means, including photocopying, recording, or other electronic or mechanical methods, without the prior written permission of the author, except in the case of brief quotations embodied in critical reviews and certain other noncommercial uses permitted by copyright law.

Illustrations by Candace Lovely
Rune Art by April Knight

Printed in the United States of America.

Library of Congress Control Number: 2022942891

ISBN   Paperback   978-1-68536-723-7
              Hardback   978-1-68536-724-4
              eBook   978-1-68536-726-8

Westwood Books Publishing LLC
Atlanta Financial Center
3343 Peachtree Rd NE Ste 145-725
Atlanta, GA 30326

www.westwoodbookspublishing.com

Frontispiece

Twenty years from now you will be more disappointed by the things that you didn't do than by the ones you did do, so throw off the bowlines, sail away from safe harbor, catch the trade winds in your sails. Explore, Dream, Discover.
—Mark Twain

Water Island. It might as well be the moons of Pluto.
Water Island. The very idea is an oxymoron.

What is an island of water? By definition, an island is *not* water. Water goes around an island. How can there be an island of water?

Illogical, basically impossible, incomprehensible.

Except in dream logic, where it makes perfect sense.

WATER ISLAND

Half from tree to ruins
ᚼᛁᛚᚹ ᚹᚱᛆᛘ ᛏᚱ�ᛏ ᛏᛆ ᚱᚢᚾᛏᛏ ᛋᛏᛆᛏᛏ

ᛒᛆᚹᚹ ᛘᛁ ᛒᛆᚹᛋ ᚢᛁᛑ ᚹᛁᚢᛏ ᛏᛆᛋᛏᛏ ᛚᛁᚹᚢᛁᚱ ᛋᚢᚹᛋ.

TABLE OF CONTENTS

1

Walk the Plank!

"Stand down, you scurvy scallywag! Lay down yer sword and swear allegiance to me pirate band, and ye live — or keep yer sword and spar with Captain Feit. I give no quarter."

Sandy felt the heat of the big man's breath on his face as he took in the barrel chest, the long arm, huge with muscle, his fist holding a sharp cutlass. The other arm had a hook. Sandy stepped back. The bear of a man strode forward and raised his sword. To either side, Sandy saw the rest of the pirate band, an assortment of gnarly men with swords held high, just inches away. Sandy held firm, head up. The pirates moved in, and the scuffle was quick, and no one was hurt. While outnumbered, Sandy held fast.

"Tie his hands behind his back. Take that map he was stealing, but leave his feet. He be walkin' the plank," said Feit, proudly puffing his chest out. "Now rig me my plank."

Two pirates leaped toward the huge landing board and swung it into place. One end on the ship, the other over water. Sandy was pushed to the plank, then prodded and poked by pirate swords . . . *onto* the plank.

"Move along, kid," snarled Captain Feit. "Let it be done. Yer fish food tonight."

A dog suddenly appeared on the deck. It looked straight at Captain Feit, head down, snarling and baring teeth. Feit raised his sword as the dog advanced. A bark, another, then in quick succession, loud barking—angry barking. One of the pirates behind the dog gave it a big kick, and the dog scurried away. "Now, kid, it's plank time. Walk." And with that, the pirates turned back to Sandy, who was bound and gagged, standing above the open ocean. A burst of wind sent the ship lurching. Sandy slipped off the plank. Falling, the wind rushing through his hair, the ocean leaped up to meet him.

This is how I die . . .

ଛ ✪ ଓ

Sandy sat bolt upright in bed. *Am I here?* He touched his arms and felt his head and hair. *Yes, this is awake. I'm here. In bed. Dreaming. Bad dreams.*

He looked out the window into the early dawn. The glint of sunlight on the ocean reminded him that he was living on an island. A tiny sliver of beach lit up by the rising sun. It all flooded back in wakefulness. *The beach, tourists, visitors, luggage—it's a hotel. No! It's Sandell's Beach Resort on Water Island, a small insignificant island off the coast of a larger insignificant island, both more than 1,500 miles from anywhere. I have a job here—a summer job. I'm making money, maybe for college one day. Maybe after high school. I'm working for Peter Sandell, who's the owner. It's a job.*

"It's a job," Mom had said back when the offer came. "Right now, you need something, and this is a job you can actually get. Nobody about to go to high school gets a summer job working on a tropical island." As Mom's car pulled up in front of Sandy's school, she continued, "You don't know your uncle Peter very well, but he's my brother, and it's incredibly kind of him to offer you a summer job, so you have to do it." She paused as she eyed the mob of kids waiting for the door to open and added, "Think of this, Sandy: a summer on your uncle's island means a break from being tormented by . . . what's that's kid's name? Joe? Moe?"

Moe Lesko, thought Sandy. *How could Mom forget?* It was a constant topic. Moe Lesko never missed a chance to torment Sandy or steal his lunch money or poke him in the ribs or shove him in the dirt. Moe never missed an opportunity to grab whatever book Sandy was reading and tear out a few pages.

Sandy had been the shortest kid in his old grade-school classes. Even in junior high, he was smaller than the other kids—an easy target for Moe Lesko and other bullies. He was always the last to be picked for teams in gym. After school, in a squabble, Sandy was always the first to be knocked down as Moe Lesko yelled, "Eat dirt, squirt."

"Besides," his mom continued, "It's an island. It might be fun."

No Moe Lesko would be fun, thought Sandy.

And now he was back in the present.

The job is dumb, simple work for a few hours a day: clean a few things, change some sheets, set up laundry, take departing guests to the ferry dock, pick up new guests, advance the laundry, and ask who needs what. New towels for Mrs. Rickerbacken in unit six. Tell Peter about the leaky pipe in unit two and about the toilet leak in unit nine . . . and about the A/C in number eight acting weird again.

It's really boring. No TV, no Internet, no games . . . Like living on the moons of Pluto.

Yet, here he was.

Some people loved the place. It was almost a private island; you only had to share it with the other folks around Sandell's resort. Palm trees, ocean, beach, snack bar . . . It amazed Sandy that people came to stay at this mini-resort on this insignificant rock. There was absolutely nothing to do. Rhone had a saying for that: "Deh all come fo' nothin'. Deh got nothin' going on and *like* nothin', or deh got too much goin' on an' *need* nothin. Either way, nothin's somethin'. Ain' dat funny . . .'"

And Sandy was here for the summer. The "off-season," whatever that might mean. Rhone had a saying for that, too.

"Dey's four seasons: tourist season, dry season, rainy, and hurricane. An' you can't shoot the tourists-dem even in deh season," Rhone had a saying for everything.

Which season is it? Must be dry. It hasn't rained since . . .

Oh, WOW, I forgot to measure the amount of water in the cistern! Yikes, how much water do we have? Uncle Peter's gonna kill me.

It was time to get up and go to work. Morning meeting. Every morning. Always at the usual seats at Rhone's Bar: Sandy, Peter, Elroy, and Ruth too. Rhone was always hovering behind the bar, listening to everything.

I wonder why the dog didn't help me, Sandy thought, his mind straying back to the dream. *What map was I stealing?*

Forget the dream. Forget the pirates. Forget it all. It's just a dream. Off to work.

᙭ ✪ ᙙ

In a cottage, not far from Sandy's room, Peter Sandell rolled over and pulled the pillow close to his chest. He snuggled up to the pillow and whispered sweet words to the cloth corner like it was an ear.

"Umm, sweetie. So warm beside you, Piper." He squeezed the pillow and started to kiss the cotton cover when wakefulness erupted.

The image of his wife lying beside him faded, and a rush of reality hit.

She's not here. But the dream was so real. She was right there, on a horse, and they were riding together, side by side, on the beach. Oh yeah, some movie we saw together. A horse story. She loved horse stories. These silly kids' stories keep invading my dreams. Even as a grown-up. Odd. Like I want to escape from here and into the stories I read as a kid. Funny.

I used to love Jamie and the Dump Truck, *Peter mused. That story was my first. I must have read it a hundred times. And* Peter Pan . . . Narnia . . . *kids' stories are so funny. People fly and animals talk.*

Well, none of that is happening here with me today. I have cottages, guests, repairs, bookings, money . . . *Oh, how I miss Piper.* Peter buried his face in the pillow, remembering being married. Having a wife. Having a best friend. Having a bookkeeper and planner. She took care of more than her half of this place. *What was it she always said? Something from Shakespeare . . . "Love all, trust a few, do wrong to none." Such a wonderful soul to lose. Now she's gone. It is just me. Alone. Doing what two people used to do and only one of us here.*

I do love this island and I did love being here with Piper. It was so exotic: a remote island, moving far from the rat race—away from winter and away from the lazy civility of the modern world. Being a couple together; having to solve stuff on our own; electrical outages, weird clients. No town water here; just rain water from the roof catchments and cisterns. Gotta rain or we're high and dry.

Yikes. Water!

Has Sandy been measuring the water in the cisterns? That kid. He's a good kid, but he's a kid nevertheless. No sense. He's a dreamer.

If I chase after him enough, he'll get the hang of being responsible. Oh, that broken storm shutter on unit six. I forgot. That hinge is outta whack . . .

And I bet someone gets locked out today and ol' Peter gotta fix a lock, or something else will knock me down.

But! I'm Peter Sandell! I always get up again. You're only defeated when you quit, and I never quit. But before you can do anything, you gotta get up, so let's go.

Peter rolled out of bed, slid into his shorts and T-shirt, slipped on sandals, and was ready for the day. He took a long hard look at himself in the mirror, lingering on the gray hair at his temples, a wrinkle beside his smile, and . . . *Oh no! There's a hair growing out of my ear. Yuck. Piper would have made a big deal out of that. She would have waxed them right away. How I miss that woman.*

2

Waterless Rock

For Sandy, the absolute best part of working on the island was going to the dock in MacPorter. Driving MacPorter was fun: it had a real clutch, four-speed shifter from a jeep, and some custom controls Ruth had devised, like a huge brake pedal you pressed for brakes but if you pushed harder with two feet, it was an emergency brake too. Pretty clever.

Every day, Sandy did a round trip to the ferry dock. Pick up new people arriving at Sandell's and take people who were leaving down. It was simple. Pick up a couple of people and their bags. Easy-peasy.

MacPorter was Ruth's idea. And Ruth wasn't like any other person Sandy had ever met. She was a tough-as-nails hard-working mechanic, and she was the entirety of the island fix-it shop. She wielded welders and wired fuse boxes. At the same time, she was charming, with her long blond ponytail and bright blue eyes. Under the grease on her face was a pretty girl. Ruth was around Peter's age—a grownup—and she had the most amazing skills with tools and machines.

Ruth had welded MacPorter into existence. Down deep, it was mostly brand-name Jeep in the engine and frame. The rest came from all kinds of cars and golf carts. The back was from a pickup truck with a bench along each side and special steps that Ruth made. The jaunty roof with fringe all around came from a golf cart. She took the driver's seat from a sports car and crafted a wooden dashboard from an old luxury car. Where the passenger seat would be, she fit in an old brass luggage rack she'd scavenged from a fancy hotel.

Sandell's Resort wasn't big—not quite a hotel and only marginally larger than a bed and breakfast. It only had twenty-four beds spread among twelve cottages. There were never more than two or three couples arriving or departing any day. Sandy loved to bop along the lane that led from the resort to the ferry dock, up the hill past Ruth's fix-it shop, then down the steep hill to the ferry dock past a long line of junk cars and trucks that had been left behind along that road. A lot of old stuff had been dropped or parked near the ferry dock and never left.

Sandy was early today so he stopped at Ruth's fix-it shop for a quick question.

Ruth looked up from a car engine with a wrench in each hand. "What'cha doin', Sandy?"

"Pickin' up newbies at the ferry dock. MacPorter's been funny. Like sputtering up the hill."

"Probably water in the gasoline. I filter that out about once a week. Maybe the spark advance on the distributor. Pop the hood."

Some hood, thought Sandy. More like . . . "Where did the hood come from?"

"I snitched it off a boat wreck that came up on the beach after a hurricane. Used to be a hatch cover, but I cut it to fit this hunk of junk."

"It's not junk," Sandy objected. "That would be old and dilapidated. MacPorter is cool. The coolest cart on this island."

"Eh, they're all junkers to me. Anything I cobble together from parts of other stuff . . . that's all mine. I can't call 'em junkers or clunkers or jalopies or wrecks. But I know under the hood it is all junk I put together and made work. That's *Ruth work*. Well, you can't call them wrecks and think people will rent them, so I needed a better name."

"Well, some of these wrecks look like they haven't run in years."

"Oh, *them*. Stuff does move in and never move out. But I like having them for parts. You never know when you're going to need a part. And on this island, there's no store selling anything, so you have to grow your own parts. When you can't find it, you don't own it."

"But do you really need ALL of these?" asked Sandy, pointing to the long line of decrepit cars and trucks.

"Those? Not mine! People left those behind. They won't pay the ferry to haul their junk to the big island, so they just leave their junk on the roadside and the people take off."

Sandy gazed along the line of decrepit cars—some without doors, others with four flat tires; pieces of pick-up trucks, and a collection of old generators. Ruth was a specialist with generators. The electricity company was notorious for system-wide failures, and when the power went out, everyone had to have some kind of backup. For most folks, it was a box of candles. For others, a bunch of batteries, flashlights, and a wind-up radio. Higher-end families had their own generator, and places like Sandell's had to have a big generator that could sustain the whole place when the power went out. Twelve cottages. twelve stoves, twelve refrigerators, twelve water pumps, twelve A/C units, plus pool pumps. That requires a lot of juice.

"I understand why you've got the generators, but some of this stuff, Miss Ruth. What are you doing with it all? Like that one," Sandy said, pointing to a very large, very rusty, power shovel that looked like it dug the Panama Canal. "Is that a steam shovel? Why is that hunk of junk here?"

"Whoa, Sandy, don't insult that steam shovel. She did hard work here. That's Alice. She came here back when Mr. Paperman first got this island. There were no roads—just ancient foot paths. He carved the roads into the hillsides and that old steam shovel did it. Alice was a workhorse; made this whole island passable. Mr. Paperman retired Alice when the road work was done and she hasn't moved since. Kinda' rusty. But moving her? No way."

"Who's Mr. Paperman?"

"First person on this island in modern times. He turned the old army buildings into a hotel. Set stuff up—roads, water. He sold building lots to some of his friends and ran a hotel in the old army buildings, refurbed as 'hotel rooms.' That's what Peter bought. He can tell you about Mr. Paperman. Paperman brought all the original heavy equipment to this island. Like that steam shovel."

"Why do you keep it?" Sandy asked. "Is Peter going to build new roads?"

"Oh, Peter," said Ruth with an air of exasperation. "He's so oblivious. Like his head is lost in a cloud all the time. He makes me crazy. He's so busy all the time. I don't think he has any idea that any of us are here. No, he's not making new roads."

"Excuse me, miss, do you rent cars?" came the voice of a day visitor, fresh off the ferry.

"Not cars," said Ruth. "I have jeeps that I make from parts—the best of every model. Custom bodies."

"Are they safe?" the visitor asked.

Sandy muffled a laugh.

"Sure, they're safe," said Ruth. "Got brakes and good steering. I'm particularly proud of the brake sets I use. All came from a guy in the states who collects brakes for jeeps. Top form. The motors are all governor-limited so nothing goes faster than 10 miles per hour. This is a little island, and you don't need to go fast. 'Cause there isn't much to see.

"Where do people go?"

"Beach mostly," said Ruth. "Rhone's Reef and Sand Bar is the only source of food on this island. That's popular. Besides, Rhone has the only working ice machine on Water Island. That's precious."

"Why is ice a big deal?"

"In this climate? Sodas get warm in minutes. It's hot. So, Rhone isn't really selling soda. Rhone sells cold, or at least, Rhone sells cool."

"Rhone *is* cool," added Sandy. "Besides, Rhone's Sand Bar is the only place on the beach. It's just a roof and the bar. Don't miss the bar, lady. It's the bottom of an old flat bottom rowboat Rhone salvaged after a storm. And the roof at Rhone's is worth a look-see. Elroy climbed palm trees, got the fronds, and wove them into a tight roof that doesn't leak. That's worth seeing."

"Is that it?" asked the lady, "a junked boat that's a bar and a roof made of leaves. That's it?"

Ruth continued, "Some folks like to explore. You can go see where the hotel used to be or where the fort used to be or where the post office used to be."

"Used to be? Is anything there?"

"No, but you can see where they used to be."

"How much for a vehicle for the day?"

"All day $40. $20 for an hour."

"Just an hour? Is that enough?"

Sandy laughed. "Lady, you can see everything on this island in about twenty minutes."

"How much for twenty minutes?"

"Same as an hour. Twenty bucks."

Just then, a modest-sized black and white dog sat down beside Sandy. He had the keys to MacPorter in his mouth.

"Oh, yikes," Sandy blurted. "Nicky knows. If you're fresh off the ferry, then my people must be waiting at the dock. Dog's right. Gotta go."

"'Scuse me, Miss Ruth," said Sandy as he jumped back in MacPorter and sped off toward the dock. "Gotta pick up the newbies." And with that, Sandy dashed off, Nicky trailing behind.

"That dog," said Ruth, almost to herself. "He knows more about what's going on than Sandy does."

ℭ ✪ ℌ

Peter was running down the fix-it list. Every day started with a strong cup of coffee at Rhone's Reef and Sand Bar and a review of the fix-it list to see what needs to be done.

Leaky pipe in unit two. Toilet leak in number nine. The A/C in number eight is weird again. It's almost like the same list every day just with different cottage numbers. Leaky pipe here, toilet drip there. A/C acting up.

Why did I take this on? Oh yeah. Live in paradise. This is paradise with endless fixing. Oh yeah, and it's the first of the month! Who is behind in the rent this month? Let's see, unit six and seven—oh and nine is behind. And has that old lady in unit seven *ever* paid anything? It was supposed to be weekly rentals. That's what Mr. Paperman said worked best.

At the closing, back when Peter bought the resort, Mr. Paperman had been emphatic: "Get 'em in and get 'em out. You want the newlyweds and nearly deads. Perfect customers. All they want is a week. If they're jerks, you only have 'em for one week. Weekly rentals, son. That's the way to run this business. And whatever you do, don't mess with Rhone. He's the only thing making any money on this island. That crazy Anguillan comes with the place. Don't mess up and lose him."

Mr. Paperman's last words at the closing. Peter owned it now. Mr. Paperman had long gone into retirement in the real world. How did he ever do all this work?

Peter looked up from his stool at the bar. Same stool as always. Corner spot looking out. Rhone behind the bar, wiping glasses. Sandwich fixin's on the counter and sodas in the cooler.

Peter got lost in his musing . . . beach, sky, and ocean . . . the ingredients of life at Sandell's resort . . . beach umbrellas, picnic tables, beach blankets . . . girls on beach blankets . . . sunbathing . . . so attractive. Oh my, look at that . . . Stop Peter! Look at the Palm trees or the ocean. Look at the wide expanse of ocean. Look at the cheerful little boats bobbing in the bay. Look at the uninhabited islands in the distance. What a vista, No wonder people come here on vacation. This is Paradise. Stop thinking about missing your wife!

Peter thought about everything *behind* the beach that was his responsibility . . . The beach bar, the showers—oh, dang; down to a trickle; mental note to change water filters. Sandell's was really nothing more than twelve cottages. Each set up for Mom and Pop and two kids. Or two couples. Or one honeymoon couple. Peter smiled at the idea of the honeymooning couples. They'd rent for a week and never be seen. Ask for nothing, no problems. At the end of a week, they were gone. That's it.

Paradise all around me but I'm responsible, thought Peter. *I'm response able. That means I gotta respond. I have no choice.*

Whoa, yikes, there is a mortgage payment due this week! And all these people are behind on rent. It's always teetering here. Teetering on the brink. I could lose the whole thing unless I come up with something.

"Rhone," Peter called from his papers. "Where's Elroy?"

"Jezsum bread, I ain' seen Elroy in days, Peter," said Rhone. "I think all'a'he people got Ka'ni'val this week on Saint Swiffins. All dem from Saint Swiffins gotta go up fo' Ka'ni'val."

"How many holidays do they have? It seems whenever stuff breaks, the fix-it guy is away, and guess who gets the job . . ."

"Peter will fix it," said Rhone as if he'd heard that line a thousand times. "Peter will fix it."

"Rhone, are you running a tab on the lady in unit seven?"

"Sure. I runs a tab on all'a'dem."

"Did unit seven ever pay you anything?"

"Lemme see. No, Peter. Her tab up a few hun'red bucks. Ain' nuttin been paid."

Peter returned to his work list as Nicky came up, wagging his tail and poking Peter's leg. Nick had a wooden key fob in his mouth. The key to unit number two. It was like the dog knew that Peter had to go fix something.

"Rhone, have you got any hot dogs for Nicky?

"Sure nuf. I got some lef'over weenies from yest'a'day."

"How about chopped liver? He prefers liver."

"Ain' no way, Peter. You wan me big up from weenies to liver? I got no chop liver for he highness, de dog," said Rhone with a laugh.

Peter took the hot dogs, held them aloft, and implored the dog. "Sit!" Nicky knew "sit" and sat down, then held out one paw, ready to shake it while looking attentively at the hot dogs. Nicky wasn't very smart—at least when it came to commands. He knew that *on command*, he had to do something. He never quite knew which command meant what. He knew "sit," and he knew "paw," but he wasn't sure which was which, so Nicky figured out that whenever there was any command, just do both. Sit and Paw. Can't miss.

But while Nicky may not have known many commands, he had an uncanny way of fetching Peter just what he needed at just the right time.

"Hey Peter," Sandy asked. "How did Nicky get his name?"

Rhone leaned in and said to Peter "Ayuh, Lawd, better make this short, mehson."

Peter started in on what was clearly a well-repeated story. "I used to have a dog just like this one. Spittin' image. Same kind. Border collie. He was the smartest dog ever. That dog would have answered the phone if he had thumbs. Smart dog, but he passed and I lamented. Right after the Hurricane, this dog shows up. He looks just like my old dog. Spittin' image. Like his spirit came back."

Rhone chimed in, "In scriptures, Nicodemus . . . he be reborn *of the spirit*. So, I says, maybe dis dog is the reborn spirit of you ol' dog. He be like Nicodemus."

"Right," said Peter. *Nicodemus, Nicky*. Whatever. It works for me. Only thing, the old dog was really smart and Nicky . . . *isn't* so smart.

"Auntie used to say 'New broom clean, but the ol' broom know the ka'nna," intoned Rhone.

"What does that mean?" asked Peter, scrunching up his face.

"Wha do you? ! You' ain' see dat?" Rhone chuckled. "You new dog do all de normal dog stuff, but you ol' dog knew stuff this one ain' git yet."

Meanwhile, Nicky didn't care and was feasting on hot dogs at Peter's feet. "Whatever, fancy name or not, he really isn't very smart."

"Awww, don't say that," said Sandy. "He brought you that key. That's pretty smart. And look how much he likes me." Nicky came up to Sandy and they exchanged greetings . . . Fur, hands, tongue licks, tail wagging. It was evident to everyone that Nicky had taken a shine to Sandy and followed him everywhere.

CR ✪ ꕔ

Hanging out at Rhone's was automatic for everyone around Sandell's. It was the only place on Water Island that served food. Rhone's Reef and Sand Bar on Water Island. Simple place. Soft drinks were made with seltzer water and syrup. Your choice of flavors. If Rhone was in a good mood, he'd "big-up" with an extra squirt of syrup. If Rhone was having an off day, not so much. Rhone had the biggest refrigerator on the island, so he had ice.

The day visitors meant Rhone had a lunch crowd of tourists every day, but by dinner time, the day-folks were gone, and just the guests and people who lived or worked on Water Island came to Rhone's for dinner. There were only a handful of regulars, and Rhone could run the place solo, which meant that Rhone was *always* there.

Saturday dinner was always special. You'd sign up at lunchtime so Rhone knew the count; then, he'd dish up his special *Ka'nibal's Feast*. All you can eat: baby back ribs, kidney beans, ears of corn, and elbow macaroni with head cheese. The salad bar had heads of lettuce with artichoke hearts in palm oil. The drink at Ka'nibal's Feast was blood orange juice, and dessert was lady fingers.

"Are you insane?" Peter bellowed when Rhone first rolled out the Ka'nibal's Feast menu. "It sounds like we're eating people."

"Funny ain' it," mused Rhone, "It's jes' food wit' people body names, and people go all crazy. It's funny to pretend. Play with a silly idea. What would a ka'nibal's restaurant have as their motto? "When you serve people, be sure to serve them with peas and rice."

In spite of his lame joke, Rhone's food was excellent, so people staying at Sandell's resort all came for dinner. Even folks off boats in the bay would come to Rhone's for his Ka'nibal's Feast.

So, it was normal, this Saturday evening in June, to have Peter sitting at his stool at the bow end of the bar where he could survey the beach and sunset. Sandy was sitting nearby, Rhone was behind the counter, wiping down glassware, Ruth was in the middle of the bar, and Elroy (along with the usual gang) was at the stern for Rhone's

Saturday Night Special. No one was surprised when a grizzled old man came into Rhone's at dinner time.

But no one was expecting the old man to speak up loudly. "Does anyone know anything about buried treasure on this island? I have a map."

3

Barney Elmer

"Does anyone know anything about buried treasure on this island? I have a dang ding map."

Peter didn't lift his head the second time the grizzled old man said it, either.

The man held up a long roll of leather as Rhone wiped the counter. "Is anyone interested in a treasure map?"

A dozen sets of eyes looked at the old man and went back to what they were doing. They thought he was a curious-looking fellow—with a wide-brimmed straw hat, a stubbled face, and a penchant for speaking out of one side of his mouth. Sandy later described him as a man with a slightly bent frame. All just a little disjointed.

Peter didn't look up. He was still absorbed in some account book. "Where'd ya' get the map?"

"Great-great uncle Buck Elmer had this. Ancient family thing. Came down from him. He got it from an old man who'd been a cook on a pirate ship. You know, colonial era . . ."

"How did a cook end up with a treasure map?" Peter still didn't look up as if he had heard all this before.

"Oh, that's part of the story, and it's the darn-gosh truth or my name's not Barney Elmer. The way the story came to me, it was a bunch of raff-riff pirates; commandeering ships, stealing gold, and doing terrible things to the passengers and crew. The band of pirates got captured, and they all got hung. But the old cook weaseled out, seein' as how he was the cook and hadn't done any of the nasty pirate stuff. That cook didn't hang, and he scooped up the map."

"So, how did it come to you?" asked Peter.

"It's just our family luck. All of us got this streak of good luck. Why I rolled three trucks in my flop-flip life and walked away without a scratch all three times. *Totaled the truck. I have the luck.* That's how come I know there's treasure. No pocus-hocus. I'm looking for a few men to go with me to this place and dig up the gold. Who's in?"

Crickets . . .

"Must be time for me to roll out the real dazzle razzle," said the old man, rolling out a large scroll of ancient leather on the counter that Rhone had just wiped, and all eyes turned to the map. Ruth leaned in, and Elroy moved beside her as Sandy and Peter leaned in. The scroll of leather had lines and words carved deep in the leather.

It was a near-perfect outline of Water Island featuring all the big rocks and bays. The shape was right. And the drawings of trees and brush matched places where they knew the underbrush was thick on the island. It was easy to identify the spot with the big tree and some words. Sandy read them aloud, *"Half from big tree to ruins . . .* What's *that* stuff? There's a bunch of stuff I can't read."

Peter was first to say, "This isn't real. Big Tree? Ruins? Gimmie a break."

Rhone looked up. "Peter, dey was a big tree up on that hill. Leas' when I was small fry . . . dem been donkey years. Up de top, I could see down all sides of de island; de whole ting, what a view. So's der *once* was a big tree up der. But how many hurricanes ago? Dem storms take it all. Hurricane . . . das *'rain goin' sideways."*

All around the bar, everyone repeated, *"Rain goin' sideways."*

On hurricanes, everyone had an opinion and a story.

"Remember, Emily, she was the first billion-dollar storm. And Hugo; he was bad."

Someone said, "Yeah. Hugo," and everyone slowly shook their heads side-to-side as if remembering the saddest day of their lives.

"Hugo took my boat away. That's how I fetched up on Water Island," said Ruth.

"Same me," came the hoarse voice of Elroy. "I blew in from St Swiffins after Hugo. Neve' lef'."

"Remember Marilyn?" Another bar voice . . .

"Yes, the power went out in September, and we didn't get power back 'til Christmas Eve. Four months—no power."

As the guys started trading storm stories about Irma and Maria, Peter and Rhone turned back to Barney Elmer's map.

"What do you think, Rhone," asked Peter. "How far is it, how bad is that road, and how wild is that part of the island?"

"Ayuh, Lawd. I don't know 'bout no *road* up der. All'a rain make dem gullies deepah. No wheel vehicle can deal with them ruts. It's all bush an' overgrowed. Ain' easy to get there. What they lookin' for? A big tree an' ruins . . .?"

"Sir! No more shally-shilly. Address this question," said Barney Elmer with his finger raised above his hat brim. "Is there a big tree on the top of that hill?"

"Well"—Rhone dragged the word out as he was thinking—"they's a lot of trees—mos'ly dinky winky. They small."

"Big?"

"Depends what you mean by big," said Rhone. "I guess some of dem is big. Sure'nuf some of dem was big. But dat's donkey years."

"Ruins?" said Barney Elmer, getting it all down to one word.

24

"Not ruins so much as piles of rock that migh'ta once been somethin' They's a lot of rocks and blocks up there. Maybe dey was pile-up like walls once."

Sandy read the words aloud again. "*Half from big tree to ruins . . .* then something I can't read. Some of this is funny writing. Either it's all rubbed down or it's not our alphabet."

"To me," Peter paused and leaned back, "this sounds crazy. You're gonna fight through thorn bushes to find a tree that isn't there, to dig for treasure that was buried four hundred years ago and was probably dug up and spent more than two hundred years ago . . . And even if the map is good, who knows that it *wasn't* dug up already? No. I'm not interested. What makes you think it's still there?"

"Lemme ax you a question, mister," Rhone leaned in and spoke. "Why it still be dere, mehson?"

"Has anyone ever heard of someone recovering any treasure here?" asked Barney, "Any record? Any stories? Not of people burying treasure. Anyone ever dug any up?"

Blank stares around the bar. No one said anything.

Rhone sliced the silence, speaking knowledgably. "We know this island was a base fo' all'a'dem pirates. Tha's fo sure. It has a great harbor. An' a pond wit' fresh water. Far from the eyes of all'dem on de big island. It's'a bes' place to stash swag . . ." he trailed off as he mused on the idea. ". . . have anyone ever *dug up* treasure here . . . it be certain dey buried some loot here . . . how come no one ain' fin' any?"

Shrugs from the gang at the bar.

Rhone stood straight upright and spoke without his Anguillan creole—and quickly, too. "I'm impressed by this map. They got all the detail; all the big rocks coming into this bay. This map is accurate. They got the high point right . . . the shape of this hill . . ."

"The map is not the territory," blurted Peter. "Doesn't matter to us if the map is right about the wrong thing. That place is all brambles and dry jungle. And why on a mountaintop? All the stories and movies have the pirates burying loot on a beach. Any treasure that might have been there is gone by now. I'm not moving," said Peter.

"I don't know Mr. Elmer, but I better stay here with my uncle Peter," said Sandy.

"I'm here," said Ruth and "Me too" said Elroy and several of the usual characters at the bar.

"Auntie used to say 'An eyeful ain' a belly full,'" as Rhone slipped back into his eastern Caribbean creole, "Dat map is jus' an eyeful. I always here. An' I stayin' here."

"So *no* one . . .?" asked Barney.

Crickets.

Barney rolled up the leather scroll and lumbered off. The next day, he was gone. He got up early, went to Ruth, rented a jeep, stashed some tools, and drove off.

WATER ISLAND

Half from tree to ruins
ᚺᛁᛁᛈ ᚹᚱᛂᚤ ᛏᚱᛂᛏ ᛏᛂ ᚱᚑᛏᛏ ᛋᛏᛂᛏᛏ

ᛒᛂᛈᛈ ᛉᛁ ᛒᛂᛈᛋ ᚑᛁᛞ ᚹᛁᚑᛏ ᛏᛂᛋᛏᛏ ᛁᛈᚢᛞᛂᚱ ᛋᚑᛈᛋ.

4

Sandy's Abduction

That night, Sandy had another encounter with the pirates.

"Stand down, ya scurvy scallywag! Lay down yer sword and swear allegiance to me pirate band and ya live, or keep yer sword and spar with Captain Feit. I give no quarter." Sandy felt the heat of the big man's breath on his face. On either side, the pirate band. Sandy held firm. The pirates moved in. The scuffle was quick.

Déjà rêvé. I've been in this dream before.

"Wait a second, Feit," came the voice of a woman standing by him. "Can he sing? We need a new voice. Before we feed him to the sharks, maybe we should do a bit of an audition."

"Aye," responded Captain Feit, "You're right, Bonny Anne; we are a voice short in the tenor range." Then turning his attention to Sandy, he bellowed, "Say, kid, can ya' sing?"

"Sing?" Sandy hadn't expected this. His hands were tied. He was standing on the plank that would take him over the side, and suddenly they wanted to know if he could sing? "What kind of singing? Why yes. YES! I was in a choir once. Church choir!"

"Lemme hear ya sing," said Feit.

Sandy cleared his throat as his mind raced to find words and a tune . . .

"Wait," said Bonny Anne. "We need to give him *our* song or we'll be hearing church music."

"Aye, she's right," said Feit, "Come on, men. Let's do some company work. We're singin' the *'Skin Ye'* song on three!" The big bear of a man turned to the band of pirates and held his arms up to direct their singing.

"Bo's'n Porklington, blow the pitch pipe."

And with that, a small fat pirate with a bald head and thick glasses came bustling forward and blew a whistle in high C.

"One, two, three," said Feit, and as if in one voice, they sang.

> We pillage, we plunder, we rifle, and loot
> We kidnap and ravage and don't give a hoot
> hey ya ho, we pirates, we will skin ye
>
> We'll cut out yer liver and give ye to hold.
> We'll kill you right now so you never get old.
> hey ya ho, we pirates, we will skin ye
>
> We're rascals, scoundrels, bloodthirsty fools
> We plunder yer booty and take all yer jewels.
> hey ya ho, we pirates, we will skin ye

"Wow," said Sandy, "that's the nastiest plan I ever heard. Do you do that stuff to people?"

"Oh! No, no, NO!" cried Feit. "Not that. We never hurt the marks. We just sing like this to scare 'em—then take all their loot. We never hurt the people. So . . . can you sing, kid?"

Sandy looked at the plank over the ship's edge. He knew where that led. On the other hand, he could sing his heart out and possibly live. Sandy puffed his chest out, took a deep breath, and delivered his version of the song he'd just heard.

The pirates all applauded.

"He's good," said Bonny Anne. "What do you think Mr. Sparhawk?"

"Got a right proper set of lungs on that lad," came the voice of the man Bonny Anne had asked.

Must be Mr. Sparhawk, thought Sandy, *and she's Bonny Anne. She sure is one tough-looking lady. The bandana hides that long black hair of hers. She could pass for a man—with the two swords on her side and all those pistols in her belt.*

Mr. Sparhawk with that eye patch and peg leg looks like he stepped out of a comic book, and he has two swords and a brace of pistols. These guys are not kidding about being armed.

Mr. Sparhawk spoke up again, "I think he has the right stuff to be a pirate. What do you say, Captain Feit? Can we keep him?"

Sandy was still bound behind, with his hands and arms pressed tightly together, and here they were talking about making him what? Their *mascot*?

"He yo," came the voice of Captain Feit. "You two—Drake and Kunkle. Stow the plank. Mr. Sparhawk, untie his bonds. We're keeping the kid. Now, kid, lemme hear you sing some more."

Sandy searched his memory but the only song he could find was one he had heard at a show . . .

> Fifteen men on a dead man's chest
> Yo ho ho and a bottle of. . .

The pirates roared with laughter as Kunkle interrupted, "No, No, kid, you sound great, but not that song. You're joining the crew of the schooner *Cruel Corsair*. You have to sing like us."

Keelhaul that scurvy sea dog,
send him down to the depths below
Make that sea dog walk the plank
with a bottle of grog and a hey ya ho

"That's the song what we would ha' sung if we'd keelhauled ya, kid. That's one of our regular songs. We do that one in four-part harmony."

"I don't get it," said Sandy. "Why do you sing?"

"It's not so much a song as a company chant," put in Captain Feit. "We sings when we're pulling on ropes and rowing. That work is all rhythmic so we got the rhythm. We use it for attunement, to get in harmony with each other. That's most of our singing.

"And we sing when we're huntin' booty," he continued. "We sing to scare the people on the prey boat. They're just marks. We make the marks think we're rough and tumble, bloodthirsty pirates. Then, we take all their stuff. Never hurt the marks we always say. Ya see, son, if you hurt people, that's evil."

Up spoke Drake to make the case. "You remember Ned Lowe? His pirate band raided the *Golden Eagle*. That man was evil. Ned killed the captain, massacred the crew, and set fire to the ship. He let the cook live, just to see him burn. Now that was an evil pirate."

"What happened to him?" asked Sandy.

"Oh, the authorities caught up with his band, hauled 'em to jail, court trial for murder. Dun hung 'em all," said Feit.

"Aye, never hurt the marks," piped up Kunkle.

"That's right," agreed Mr. Sparhawk. "No nasty crime."

"See, that's why we work on our singing," said Captain Feit. "Gotta all know the words and the tune and sing, so they can tell we're serious."

A voice came from high in the crow's nest, "Ahoy! Captain! Bounty ship to the starboard bow."

"Where's me spyglass, Porklington?" shouted Feit, grabbing his glass from the Bo's'n.

"Aye, looks like the King's treasury barque sailing alone." said Feit, squinting into his spyglass. "Fat birds are easy prey. This must be my day."

"Get close-hauled," yelled Bonny Anne to the helmsman. "That treasury barque is flying square sails and struggling ta' windward. We can sail a close reach and catch that old tub with ease."

"As the lady says," agreed Feit. "We sail on orders of our pilot Bonny Anne. And I shall command the boarding party."

"Are ye all in?" she yelled.

"Aye-aye" came the voices of all the mates.

"What do you want me to do," asked Sandy.

"Well join us, of course," said Feit as he turned to the band. "Men! Everyone practice. They don't call me the *King of the High Cs* for nothing," said Feit.

As the pirate sloop approached the barque, Sandy could see the name on the transom; *Midas Touch . . .*

Turns to gold. That's interesting.

Then, Sandy scrambled over to join the band, standing by Mr. Sparhawk as he got up his courage to ask, "Who's really in charge? Is it Mr. Feit or Bonny Anne?"

"Aye, kid. It ain't like that wit' pirates. No one is all in charge like they can just do anything. This is a democracy. We vote the boss in, and we can vote them out. Secret ballots and open count. We do democracy right. Ain' no pilot can beat Bonny Anne."

"Aye," added Drake. "She's the best on the seven seas. Everything a woman should have; navigation skills, management, perseverance. She passed all the pirate tests for skills and competence with flying colors. She's best-in-class."

"What about Mr. Feit? "

"The captain?" said Mr. Sparhawk with an astonished look on his face. "No one do it like he do. He's the best. Best of 'em all. You'll see. Watch how he do this."

The pirate band was tuning up. Someone had a fife, another had a concertina, and most had noisemakers or rattles. All of them had weapons, either in their belts or in their free hand. As they got into close range, they began to sing. Then, a blast sounded from their cannon across the bow of the *Midas Touch*, and a couple of choruses of their bloodthirsty song later, everyone on the *Midas Touch* raised their hands in surrender.

"Make quick with the boarding pikes, me hearties," bellowed Feit as he stood astride the main hatch amidships. The crew used the long-hooked poles to grab the gunnel of the *Midas Touch* and pull her close by.

Feit yelled to his boarding party. "Ready to board!" Twelve pirates leaped across the space between the ships, all armed to the teeth with cutlasses, sabers, dirks, daggers, boarding axes, and pikes. They looked like looming death to the passengers and crew aboard the *Midas Touch*.

Once aboard, the pirate's cut the halyards on the *Midas Touch*, and her sails came crashing down. Ropes were passed, and the ships were tied together. Between the two ships, the landing plank rose into place like a highway. Captain Feit, with lit fuses in his beard making a cloud of smoke, strode across the plank, and stepped aboard the *Midas Touch*.

"Good day to all you good fellows and ladies. Thank you for your kind welcome. I am Captain Phinneas Feit, and we're the crew of the *Cruel Corsair*. We came for your loot, and if you make haste and deliver, we'll spare all your lives. We're proper gentlemen, pirates. Not a hair shall be hurt if you do as I say."

"What want ye, Mr. Feit?" came a voice from the captured crew. "I am Captain of the *Midas Touch*. We gave thee fair passage to board. Please harm none of my passengers or crew. We offer no resistance."

"Porklington, where's the list?" yelled Feit as he turned to the little pirate man with the bald head.

"Here, sir." said the boson, scurrying up to the captain.

"Aye," Feit bellowed. "Read it, bo's'n." Then, Feit kept talking. "We be needin' all yer gold, silver pieces, and gems.

"My apologies, Mr. Feit,' came the voice of the prey ship's captain. "We carry no gold. *Midas Touch* is a passenger ship. We have no gold."

"Aye," said Feit, "That's what they all say." Then in a squeaky voice. "We have no gold." Then roaring to Kunkle, "Kunkle, go to this Captain's quarters. Find his chest of gold and be sure to check all the usual hiding places. Mr. Sparhawk, you examine the cargo hold for rum."

"Now, then, my good man," said Feit. "Then, we be takin' all yer rum, whiskey, tobacco, and coffee."

"And see if they have any tea," came the voice of Bonny Anne from the deck of the *Cruel Corsair.*

"And do you happen to have any tea?" repeated Porklington, and then reading from the list. "And if you please, any soap, candles, thimbles, thread, frying pans, or kettles."

"Yeah, all that too," echoed Captain Feit.

"Yes, yes, whatever you want," came the voice of the *Midas Touch* captain. "Quick, gather up all our provisions these men want: candles, thimbles, whatever."

Kunkle appeared from the rear hatch, hauling a chest that certainly seemed to be weighty. "Yo Captain, this be full of coinage," said Kunkle.

"Haul that chest aboard the *Cruel Corsair* and stow it in my cabin," Feit answered.

As they were hauling kitchen kettles and bags of grain over to the *Cruel Corsair,* the one called Drake came up from below decks carrying two cases of rum bottles followed by Mr. Sparhawk with one of the ladies thrown over his shoulder. Sparhawk was headed toward the plank, taking her aboard, while she was kicking and struggling.

"Now, wait a minute, Mr. Sparhawk," came the voice of Bonny Anne. "You may *not* bring a woman aboard our ship. Can't break the rules. It's in the Articles. We all swore . . ."

Mr. Sparhawk responded, "'T'ain't no prohibition on taking ladies . . ."

"Oh, yes there is," responded Bonny. "It's in the Articles. Bo's'n Porklington, fetch the Articles of Agreement and read 'em here."

The small pirate scurried up and drew a document out of his leather pouch, adjusted his thick glasses, and began reading the titles of the different sections of the pirates' Articles of Agreement.

"Let's see here now," he muttered as he riffled through the pages of the thick folio. "Every man has a vote in all affairs . . . Election of Captain Feit . . . Election of Miss Bonny as pilot . . . There's a section here on share of plunder, share of gold, share of rum. Rule for keeping pistols clean and fit for service. No hitting, no hitting back . . . No gambling . . . No stealing . . . No smoking in bed . . . Lights out at 8 p.m. . . . Musicians rest on the Sabbath . . .

"Ah here it is: *If at any time we meet with a prudent Woman, any man that offers to meddle with her, or carry her to sea without her consent shall suffer present death.*"

"That's the section," said Bonny Anne, "excuse me, milady, but are you consenting to accompany this man aboard our ship?"

"No, you brute," she said, striking Mr. Sparhawk on the side of his head. "Unhand me."

"Sorry, Mr. Sparhawk, but you canNOT kidnap ladies and bring them onto this ship. That's our rules. Of course, you can suffer present death. We have a plank . . ."

Mr. Sparhawk looked down, lowered the young lady back until she was standing and bowed while he apologized. "My deepest apology, milady. I beg your comfort if I have in any way injured you."

"Apology not accepted, you brute," said the lady as she reorganized her dress and hat and stomped away.

"See, we aims to be gentlemen about this piracy business," said Feit. "Just take the money and be polite to the people. That's what I says."

Just then, a dog sat down beside Sandy and held out its paw. "Look captain," said Sandy, "A dog. And it likes me. He brought his leash in his mouth. He wants me to take him for a walk. What do you say, Captain Feit? Can we keep him?" asked Sandy.

"No rules against dogs here," said Bonny Anne. "But ask the people on *Midas Touch* if you can keep their dog."

Sandy piped up as he turned to the captain of the *Midas Touch*, "Is it ok if we take the dog?"

Their captain answered, "Please, please, take anything you want. Just don't kill us!"

Feit responded: "Oh no. No one getting killed. Cute doggie," said Feit, "Can we take the doggie?"

"Go." said the captain, "Just go. Please spare us any pain."

The pirates returned to their ship with the loot, with the dog, and with*out* the lady. Ropes were cast off and the pirates all tipped their hats to the people on the *Midas Touch*, as they sailed away, leaving that ship adrift and without provisions.

"Is that all you do? Steal food and stuff and damage the ship?" Sandy asked.

"No, no, son, we just helped ourselves to some necessary supplies, and we didn't a hurt nobody."

"What do you do with the loot?"

"Well," said Feit, "we drink the rum and eat the food and mend everything with their needles and thread, and then go to a handy island and bury the loot."

"Wait, so you steal all the gold and then just bury it?"

"Yup. Well, we really can't use the jewelry so much. No way we can sell it. Gold is handy in port but it's heavy, and our boat has'ta be light to catch our prey. All'a we pirates cannot just saunter into town an' deposit in a bank. So what are we gonna do with gold coins? We burys it."

Feit continued, "There are some choice islands 'round these parts. Uninhabited. All private-like and no one knows we stashed our loot there. It's all 'bout findin' the right spot that's easy to find again. Make a map. Save it. Sometimes we digs up some coins and buy things. Sometimes we're loaded with loot and bury more in the same place. That's our kinda bank. We have chest upon chest of loot in some places."

"But wait a minute Mr. Feit, you still stole all this stuff. Not just the gold, you stole kettles, pins, needles, wooden spars, all their food. That's illegal."

"Better than killing them, I always say," lamented Feit.

"But you're still a bunch of crooks. Stealing is wrong."

"Ok, men," bellowed Captain Feit. "This kid is going berserk. Outta control. Singing or not, you're done. Seize him."

In a flash, Kunkle, Drake, and Mr. Sparhawk grabbed Sandy and bound him with rope and pushed him out onto the plank.

Déjà rêvé. I've been here before, thought Sandy, suddenly aware that he was dreaming. But it's different. The dog is here. He's standing beside me. He's growling at the pirates. He's snarling at them. Holding them off . . .

A burst of wind. The ship lurched. Sandy slipped, and he found himself falling. The wind was rushing through his hair. The ocean was leaping up to meet him. It was now that he di—

No! He hit the water! He was *underwater.* The dog was here. Beside him. It was Nicky with a leash in his mouth. Sandy's ropes fell away. Nicky pulled Sandy to the surface, soon swimming beside Sandy, bobbing him along, sometimes pushing. Nicky got Sandy to an island . . . beach . . . sand . . . palm trees . . . a map . . .

Blink. Blink. Awake.

5

Falling or What . . .

Sandy was awake. In bed. On Water Island. Sandell's Resort. No pirates. No gold.

Sandy stared at the ceiling for just a moment then remembered. *This is Saturday; I have the morning off. I can roll over and go back to . . . Sleep! More sleep would be good but not that pirate place. Where to go this time . . .?*

ଓ ✪ ଈ

Sandy found himself on a rocky path in the mountains, walking toward a tiny cottage nestled between the mountainside and the spires and pinnacles that lined the canyon. High up in the thin crisp spring air with a hint of pine and flowers. There were birds somewhere.

I know this place, thought Sandy as he took in the scene. *I've been here in my dreams. It's Knight School.* Sandy flashed back to this place. A bunch of kids like me, sitting around the front porch of this old house in the mountains talking about dreams.

If you've never read any of Sandy's other adventures, he always visits Knight School. Nestled in his dreams, Knight School is a place where people go to learn about their dreams. It only exists in dream space, so don't go looking for it in the *WakeWorld*.

And Knight School means teachers, and for Sandy, his teacher was Reed Sundance.

Where's Reed? thought Sandy. *Such a strange man—so thin and so tall, like the smallest amount of body in which a human spirit could reside. Thin, high voice that sounds like wind in trees. He's strange, but the whole place is strange.*

Strange things can happen in dreams. And because this is dream space, strange things did happen. Sometimes, the walls would change color or a frog would wander through or thunder would pierce the quiet. And oftentimes, the other kids would be people he met here before.

Sandy sailed down the path toward the little house amid the rock spires. The porch with rough wooden rails all around, comfy chairs, rocking chairs, and piles of pillows was a perfect place for a small group to sit in a circle and talk about dreams.

"I know you," stammered Sandy. "Reed. You're Reed Sundance. I've seen you before in my dreams, haven't I?"

"Yes, welcome back, Sandy. We've been waiting for you to return."

He looked around at the people in the circle. Some were faces he'd seen before, and others were new.

"Why am I here?" Sandy asked as he sat down in a comfy chair.

"We all want to know that," said Reed.

"I mean at this *school*."

"Sandy, you were nightmaring yourself. Again."

"But why are *you* here, Reed? Why is this *place* here?"

"To reconnect you to yourself." Reed relaxed and spoke in a low solemn tone. "I find so many people who are disconnected lost in life, from their dream life, and unaware of their inner being. I created Knight School to reconnect people to their dreaming mind.

"We all know that *inside* there's more here than just meat and bones. Yet, none of us knows exactly what it is. We use folk names; *spirit, soul, light within*, lord . . . You call it what you like. That part of us speaks in dreams."

Reed continued and the kids in the circle all leaned in to listen to his words of wisdom. "Dreaming is our earliest form of thought. It's ancient. Yet, we ignore it, let it crumble in disuse—broken, forlorn, left in the dustbin of night. Yet, it's still there; indomitable.

"Your dreaming mind insists on being heard. Dreaming is what's left of the way we used to think before we had language . . . before we named time . . . before we had a way to name things. We had dream thinking all the time. Our deepest ancestors had *dreaming* as their normal thinking. It's old. It's deep. Yet, most of us ignore it. We pay no attention. Not only do we ignore dreams, but we don't think they're connected with our lives. We're disconnected."

Reed turned to Sandy and spoke more pointedly. "We saw you having your falling nightmare. Out of control, were you?"

"Every time I meet those pirates, I fall off the plank," said Sandy. "Even when they're being nice to me. I end up falling off that plank. In one dream, we were all chummy and sweet like a band of brothers, and I still slipped off that plank and fell. I always wake up just before I hit the water. Except once . . ."

"I had that one too," said a kid Sandy knew. His name was Mars. "Only without the water. I'd fall out of a tree and wake before I hit."

"I had that falling dream too. I'd fall fast and wake up just before I hit. That was so scary," said another kid.

Reed asked all around, "Do any of you fly?"

"I do sometimes," said a girl Sandy didn't recognize. "I fly into the clouds. For me, it's like swimming in the air."

Others spoke up:

"I flew once too. I put my arms out, and the wind just picked me up. And another time, I wasn't really flying; it was more like running up invisible stairs."

"I fly in my dreams by jumping a couple of times, and on the third jump, I take off. Then I'm like Ironman. I put my arms down, palms facing the ground, and I close my eyes and concentrate on lifting."

"I used to just hover, and then once, a storm came and blew me away—sideways. That's how I'd make lateral moves."

"This is weird. I have this strange position that lets me fly. Like I'm sitting in a chair but I can put my hands below my bottom, make a tight grasp, and push upward. It's how I fly."

"That's so cool," said Mars. "It's like you're carrying yourself . . ."

"Exactly," said Reed, who then asked, "Have any of you changed falling into flying?"

"Oh, yeah. I did that," said Mars. "I was falling and about to hit the rocks when I swooped and skittered along the ground for a while before I soared up into the air. I stopped having the falling nightmare right after I went bungee jumping in the waking world. I was so scared.

But I came out fine. You can't be scared of something you've done and survived."

Reed asked, "Have you ever flown in your *WakeWorld* life? Not in an airplane but flying your body in the real world? Anyone?"

All around the circle, heads were shaking side-to-side. No.

"Of course you have," said Reed. "Think like a baby. Mama picked you up from a crib and flew you over to the changing table for your diaper. Then, Mama flew you to the highchair or the play place or the stroller. You spent most of your baby era being flown around. All of that is still in you—*deep* in you. Your body remembers flying. So find that deep memory and map it onto your today self.

"During the day today, stop what you're doing and be a baby again and remember how it felt to fly. Remember our focus ritual: Stop what you're doing and cleanse your mind. Be. Here. Now. Then, press the palms of your hands together, and feel them touch and not slip or flow into one another. Clap twice. Think about when you flew as a baby. Then, get back to work."

Just as Reed finished, a dog came running up on the porch and walked right over to Sandy. He sat and put out his paw and Sandy knew at once that it was Nicky. And in his mouth, he was carrying a blindfold, reminding Sandy it was time to wake up.

Reed was delighted to see Nicky too. "He's your dream dog, Sandy. He'll be there for you in your dreams and maybe he'll fly with you.

"All right, everyone. Dog's right, gotta go," Reed said in a high reedy voice. "It is time to return to *WakeWorld*. Everyone, get into a comfortable position . . ." Reed began a slow drone of word patter that led everyone to the drowsy zone between dreaming and waking as their bodies returned to the waking world.

Reed intoned,

> "Relax deeply and calmly.
> Let your eyes gently close now
> Relax as relaxation drifts all over you

Relax as it laps gently through your muscles
Relax as it sweeps in deep rest
Feel the wonderful release flowing through your body
Feel the wonderful release flowing through your
mind . . .
Hover there . . . Hover there
Now rise up.
Come up,
Rising quickly up, up, up into the *WakeWorld*."

Blink, Blink, Awake.

ᘓ ✪ ᘏ

A glint of sunlight on the beach and the gentle sound of waves lapping at the sand. A tropical island. Beach, tourists. Yikes. Sandell's Beach Resort. Rhone's Reef and Sand Bar, Elroy, Ruth, Peter.

Yikes! How late is it? I overslept. Oh wait . . . Day off.

What was that dream? Falling . . . Flying . . . Look at your hands and remember . . . be a baby flying. What craziness. I saw that stupid map yesterday and had a dream about pirates and buried treasure. Then I'm talking to some guys about falling and flying. At least the dog was on my side this time. The dog. I love the way my dreams are populated with dogs. Eh, it's just a dream. Dismissed. What's Peter always say? 'But first, ya gotta get up.'

Sandy rolled out of bed, put on his shorts and T-shirt, and slipped into his flip-flops. He was ready for the world. Day off. Still, he needed food, so out the door he 0went, on his way to Rhone's where a morning meeting might be happening anyway—and food.

Peter was on his usual stool at the bow end of the boat hull that made the bar of Rhone's Reef. He was deep in coffee, tallying figures and working on getting ready to start thinking about writing a list of things to do.

"I don't get it, Rhone," said Peter. "Only twelve cottages. How come something is always busted?"

"Yah, daddi. Rust run fas'er in paradise. Chaos come quicker," said Rhone."

"Lemme see. I fixed the leaky pipe in unit two yesterday, and today it's leaking again. Toilet leak in nine. Got that. The A/C in number eight . . . Did Elroy fix that?"

"Elroy ain' here."

"Rhone, Where's Elroy? Elroy is my master fix-it man, the guy who's supposed to do this stuff. Where is he today?"

"He ova dere, Saint Zenobia. Dey have de festival fo' Saint Zenobia on he islan'."

"There's a Saint Zenobia?"

"They get to deh en' o' deh alphabet and still got lotta names lef' over, so dey got more saints dere."

"How come there are so many saints, Rhone?"

"Man, in the Caribbin' we got lotsa saints. We got islands that's saints, cities that's saints, mountains that's saints. We got saints in Spanish and French. We got one bunch a'islands named for Saint Ursula and a *thousand* virgins. Tha's a lotta saints."

"That's a lot of *virgins*," came a voice from the stern end of the bar.

Peter asked, "So how come there's no saint for fixing stuff at Sandell's Resort. And what happened with the A/C in number eight?"

"Oh, dat lady was like an emergency. I call Missy Ruth. Dat Ruth kin fix anythin'."

"Yes, and she doesn't take off for Saint 'Zoobia's' Day."

Peter surveyed the beach. Maybe twenty people. Half of them women. Peter stared blankly at the scene, his coffee cup poised halfway to his mouth as he lost awareness of what he was doing . . .

"Peter, you starin' at the women ag'in mehson," muttered Rhone.

"Yeah, I guess I was. So pretty. Ah, bah, this place is endless work. Same stupid list every day."

Peter shrugged, got up and headed out of Rhone's bar.

ℭℛ ✪ ℬ

Knock, knock on the door of unit two. "Hello, I'm here to fix the leak."

Even before the door opened, the voice rang out "Oh thank goodness. I just got here today, and I've never been to a place like this before, and I can't tell you what's wrong with the water. It's all over the floor. Oh my God, it just keeps coming and coming."

"Good afternoon," said Peter, stepping inside. The woman was in her twenties and unusually good-looking. And Peter was, for a moment, stagestruck. He forgot what he was there to do until she said, "Were you going to fix the leak?"

"Oh, yes. That's it." Peter entered the bathroom, and there was a puddle on the floor in front of the sink. He ducked his head under the sink, identified the source of the leak, and banged his head getting up. Rubbing his head, he said, "Easy fix. I'll just be a minute with my wrench." The woman stood at the doorway watching Peter as he got a wrench from his toolbox and returned under the sink.

"Do you work here a lot?"

"I'm the owner," said Peter.

"You own this place? All of it?"

"Aye," said Peter while tugging on a wrench, tightening the joint on the leaky pipe.

"All of it? Beach too?" she said again getting closer to where Peter was working and leaning in for a close look. "You must be incredible."

There came a knock at the door. "Peter. There's a leak in #6." It was Sandy.

"Tell Elroy?" yelled Peter.

"He's gone."

"What happened to the A/C in unit 8?"

"Oh, Ruth fixed it."

"Oh, yeah. Rhone told me. That Ruth, she can fix anything. Ok. I'll get to unit six as soon as I finish here. And Sandy, get a mop and bucket and come get this puddle."

"What a remarkably responsible man you are," the woman said. "Do you do all the repairs?"

"No. I have staff who are supposed to fix things, but somehow the fix-it guy is always away and I get stuck making sure it is all right. Sandy will be right back up to mop up the puddle."

"I can't really tip an owner, but how about a big hug for coming so quick." She wrapped her arms around Peter and pressed her head against his shoulder. Peter welcomed the warmth but had no idea how to respond.

"Will I see you at dinner?"

"Yes, probably."

 C3 ✪ ಐ

Sandy looked for Ruth at Rhone's after he finished mopping up the puddle in unit two.

"Did you meet the new lady in unit two?" he asked.

"No. Who is she?"

"Like a model or something. Maybe on TV or in the movies. Such a face, and—"

"Did Peter meet her?" Ruth asked with a wry hint.

"He was fixin' something in the bathroom, and when I went back with the mop, he had that vacant look in his eyes—you know, like, thunderstruck. The way he looks when he's on his stool here lookin' at the day visitors all over the beach. You know, *that look*."

"Oh, Peter. He's always looking at the girls. Peter has dreams about some princess finding him here."

Rhone leaned into the conversation and said, "Ayuh Lawd, like God gonna drop Miss Right outta'a helicopter and she gonna walk right 'cross de beach and fall in he arms. Dream come true."

"You think so?" asked Sandy.

Ruth answered, "Peter doesn't know what he's looking for. He's lost. Lost in his dreams."

"Das funny." Rhone was setting up lunch. "He's always harpin' about how stupid dreams is. But he got dream stories all'a time. Dreaming 'bout kid books and t'ings. I heard him rail about that steam shovel story so many times. He always pushin' it off, but he livin' in he dreams. Da badd."

"I think they're great fun," said Sandy. "I have times I go back to the same dream and pick it up where I left off. Other times, I go to all new places."

"Sandy, you getting' lost in *yo'* dreams. How many times you late to a meetin' 'cause you sleepin'?" asked Rhone.

"I think dreams matter," said Sandy, avoiding the subject of his lateness. "I work on them. I try to make sense of 'em and fix whatever is making nightmares. You do it every night too, ya know."

"Come on, Sandy. That's zany,' chuckled Ruth. "No one really believes that dreams are talking to us in any kind of useful way, right Rhone?"

"Whoa, don' go knockin' dreamin'," Rhone hurled back. "I think they rich with portents 'n' visions. It say in scripture 'bout you ol' men havin' dreams an' you young men seein' visions.' Looks to me like you dreamin' mind is like a garden. It got fertile ground for new things to grow. But 'you only reap what you sow' that's what Auntie use' ta say. If Peter wanna wallow in he sadness, then he gonna dream sadness or he gonna thrash around lookin' for what *used* to give him pleasure. Kids books and steam shovels."

Ruth popped in. "Remember that time Peter was talking about how Piper told him in a dream that she saw him getting hit with a falling coconut tree, and just a day or two later, Peter had a near miss with a fallin' coconut tree. That really shook him up."

"Yes," Rhone replied. "Tha's a dream that came true. No wonder Peter freaked out."

"Who *is* Piper?" Sandy asked with his wrinkled brow.

"Oh, you don't know Peter much from before." Rhone's eyes dropped. "Piper was he wife."

"Peter was married?" Sandy was surprised.

"He was—once," Rhone recited the memory. "He don' talk 'bout that much at all. Sad. Deh was so happy when deh first come he-ya. Young couple, doing somethin' darin'—adventuresome—an' heard de call of a tropical island and figured dey could manage. She ran de books and de money. He took care of de people. Peter 'n' Piper—they was a dream team. Den she got sick. Dey went to the mainland for doctorin' and she ain' fix. When he come back, he all alone. He been los' ever since . . . can' decide if he mournin' he los' wife or chasin' some new girl, looking for his old love or what . . ."

"He sure is talking and acting lonely," chimed in Ruth.

"I sure wish I could dream up some new love for Peter," sighed Rhone and he turned slowly, wiped the counter, and cleaned up glasses where people left them. He tidied up the sandwich fixin's and went back to check the ice machine.

You'd think he'd notice me, thought Ruth.

Out of the long silence, Sandy looked down and caught a glimpse of his hands. He stopped, looking more closely. Is this *WakeWorld* or *DreamWorld*?

Hands. Remember flying. Flying as a baby. Flying. Look at his hands and fly . . . flying over Water Island . . . flying over the high point . . . Flying over a map . . . Barney's map. Then, his mind snapped back. What happened to Barney?

Sandy looked up, saw Ruth, and asked, "What would it take to go see how Barney is doing? What would it take to go there?"

"You can take MacPorter. Peter won't care. It can make that trip. Easy. As soon as the road gets impassable, then park and walk. Shouldn't be more than a mile or so to walk . . . uphill . . . through thorn bushes. By the way, he never came back with my jeep. So, keep your eye out for my machine."

"What do you mean he never came back?"

"He never brought back my jeep. Nor any tools."

"He may be up der still," offered Rhone.

"So, what do I need so I can check up on him?" asked Sandy.

"Hiking boots, wide-brim hat," said Ruth but she was interrupted.

Rhone blurted, "Better take a shovel to dig up *yo' share* of de big treasure."

"Do you really think there's gold up there?" asked Ruth.

Rhone chortled as he said, "Jezsum bread, mehson. He pro'lly up on that hill goin' crazy, diggin' holes, lookin' for somethin' ain' dere. Auntie used ta say, 'All crab fin' deh own hole.'"

"Yeah, Sandy. Better take along a straitjacket," added Ruth. "That guy was a loose cannon down here, but after a few days on that hill, in the sun, going crazy, digging holes . . . he may be crazy . . ."

"Worse," said Rhone. "He may be he dead. Done dug he own grave."

That hadn't occurred to Sandy. No matter how much of a lure the treasure might be. Crazy or dead was not so inviting. Sandy wandered back to his room, thinking, Crazy or dead . . .

6

Look at Your Hands!

Sandy was on the pirate's plank—yet again. Feit was yelling something about scurvy scallywag. The guys were singing their nasty song. One voice sang the lead line, and all the pirates responded, thumping their feet on the plank with each "fish food, fish food." And all of them thumping the plank made it shudder and jump.

> Now walk the plank, and now you're screwed
> Fish food fish food.
> The fish be ready with beer they brewed
> Fish food fish food.
> Feed the fish and don't be rude
> Fish food fish food.
> They eat ya raw, they eat ya crude

Fish food fish food.
Yer life is over, you now conclude
Fish food fish food.
Yer trash to us, ye ballyhoo
Fish food fish food.
The fish will eat ya, they're not shrewd.
Fish food fish food.
Yer in the ocean, already stewed
Fish food fish food.
They'll nibble yer timbers until yer chewed.
Fish food fish food

Responding to a puff of wind, the ship lurched, and after one thump too many . . . Sandy was falling again. The wind in his hair, the ocean looming, Sandy thought, *I've been here before. Déjà rêvé.*

The dog! The dog is here! The dog had a paw out. Sandy touched the dog's paw and slowed. And suddenly, he wasn't falling. And he wasn't hitting the ocean either. Sandy looked around. He was hovering, floating above the plank. The pirates were looking at him with faces distraught, tied in knots like they were seeing a ghost or a demon.

Hovering. Hovering . . . then Nicky, rolled over in the air and, began to slide sideways. And Sandy, all limbs outstretched, started to slide sideways, too. *Floating sideways beats hitting bottom!*

Sandy held his hand out to the dog's paw, grasped Nicky's paw, and then, with paw in hand, he thought, Look at your hands. Be Here Now. Fly.

Suddenly for Sandy, it was like Peter Pan, Superman, Thor, and Captain Marvel all at once. Sandy was flying. Flying! He had to try everything: tumble in the air, go fast, go slow, hover, fly with the dog, fly beside the dog. Under, over; rolling, spinning.

Wait! What did Reed say? "Go somewhere worth going."

Of course, thought Sandy, *somewhere worth going*, and he called aloud, "Come on, Nicky. Let's fly to Knight School . . ." And because this is dream space, they flew there in an instant.

I know this rocky path in the mountains. I've been to this tiny cottage, high in this canyon. There is thin crisp spring air and the smell of pine and flowers. There are birds somewhere. I'm at Knight School, thought Sandy. He floated himself down the path and stepped down onto the wooden porch with the circle of kids. Same as before. Some he knew. Some were fresh faces.

Nicky took off to sniff things. Sandy took a few steps toward the rocking chair.

The guy named Mars spoke up as soon as Sandy sat down. "Did you hit the water or wake up?

"Neither," said Sandy. "I saw Nicky's paw, and I saw my hand, and I touched Nicky, and I stopped falling. How did I do that? I wasn't in control of that?"

"Your dreaming mind doesn't need you to be in control," Reed said, gently opening his eyes. "You heard us talk about looking at your hands and flying, so the idea was planted in your mind. Your dream mind figured it out in its own way. Your dream mind even sent Nicky to be with you when you fly. He's your flying partner. You can do anything in your dreams."

The kid named Blake asked, "But how do you make things happen in your dreams? You make it sound like you're running the story while I experience my dream as if it's happening to me. Not like I run it."

"Yeah," said Mars. "My dreams are like movies, and I'm just watching. How do I change the action?"

Reed was ready. "Be careful. We don't want to *make* our dreams do things. We want our dreams to invent new things and try new ideas. If you think that something could happen, then your dream mind might try it. You feed your dreaming mind ideas by day and it plays with them by night.

"So, how do we get those day ideas to be part of our dreaming mind?" asked Mars. "I don't think I know any way to feed ideas to my dreams."

"Yes," replied Reed, speaking slowly. "Everything you do, say, or receive is fodder for dreams. So, what are you putting in you? What are you filling your mind with? TV? Video games? Violence? Or what? Get presence of mind. That's real magic."

"Presents of mine?" asked a girl sitting to Sandy's right . . .

"No," said Reed, "*presence of mind.* Be present."

"Presence? Presents? Sounds the same to me. But I still don't know how to get presence in my mind," said Mars.

Reed closed his eyes and slowly reopened them. "No one knows exactly how we pay attention, but you *pay* attention. It costs you. You give a little of yourself to pay attention. Do this! Stop! Take a mental snapshot: this venue, this situation, right now. Make yourself pay attention to where you are and what you are seeing. Be. Here. Now. Right here on this porch and in this instant. Put your hands together palm to palm and press them together. In dream space, they will flow into one another. In *WakeWorld* they will feel the other hand pressing back. Now ask yourself, 'Is this real?' Question your reality. 'Am I awake or dreaming?' Right here in this instant."

Reed waited for a moment as all the kids in the circle tried various things as they tried to pay attention to the instant.

"Did I just push my hand through my other hand?" asked Blake. "Yikes."

"Oh, yow, I just pushed my hand through the wall," said Kat.

"Woah, the seat isn't holding me up," interjected Mars.

And Reed was concerned and called them back, "Everyone come back to right here and right now, or we'll all dissolve into our own dreams again."

As they all resumed their places around the circle, Reed continued. "In waking time, stop and look at your hands. They're your trigger. Get presence of mind, then look up and take it all in. Right now. Every sense. All mindful. Focus. Give—right now—100%."

"So, do I *do* anything when I'm stopping to pay attention? What do I do?" asked Mars.

"Do?" asked Reed with one eyebrow up, "Do? It is not about doing. It's about attending. It's about being right here and right now. Paying attention is the something you do."

Sandy felt a cold nose touch his arm and saw that Nicky was there.

"Dog's right. Gotta go," said Sandy to Reed. The dog held out a paw. Something glittering was in his mouth. Sandy touched the paw, and they started to float up from the porch, out into the air, and high above the shack.

Far behind, Sandy could hear Reed calling, "Go somewhere worth going."

High above the Knight School canyon, Sandy could feel the cool air, and with Nicky by his side, he was ready to fly anywhere . . . but where?

Of course. Find the treasure! Go to the place. Where is the map? I saw it once. I'm flying. I must be dreaming. It is in my dream space. Everything is in dream space. All I have to do is remember it. Think about it. I can find the map.

Sandy looked down at the ocean and Barney's map unrolled below him. He was flying over Barney's map, circling around, looking at the contours of the land. The map turned transparent. Seeing the real island through the map, Sandy flew down through the transparent map and landed on top of the island's highpoint. There was a great wide plain at the top and a big tree and a pile of old stone blocks from some kind of collapsed tower or walls. Captain Feit and his pirate band were digging. Mr. Sparhawk, Kunkle, and Drake were leaning heavily into their shovels. Porklington was there, making a map of the place.

But how many holes!?! So many holes. Which one has the treasure? What is that huge rock at the opposite end of the plain from the ruins? Why is the bo's'n over there at that huge stone? What is he doing? What are those marks on the stone?

Blink. Blink. Awake

⌒⭐⁊

"What's the weather forecast?" Peter asked Rhone.

"I heard the Good News Guy this morning," said Rhone. "You'd ha thunk he got a recordin' of de weather. Always de same," Rhone continued imitating the weatherman's voice. "'Full sunshine today, high around 82, and with the wind chill it feels like 82.' Then, he chuckled and went on, 'Overnight low might get down to 80. Northeast wind, five knots, possible hit-or-miss showers.' An if'n you listen all careful-like, he chuckles at de same spot every day. Mus' be a recordin'. De weather neba changes, why should de weather guy change?"

"Yeah, the weather never changes," came the voice of Ruth from the stern seats at the end of the bar.

"Hit or miss showers. Sounds like the story of my life," came another voice from the stern end.

"So, no rain, right Rhone?" asked Peter.

"Rain? Wha do you? You be dreamin', Peter. You gonna hav'ta squeeze dat blue real hard to get rain out."

In the second of silence, Sandy jumped in. "Hey Peter, you may be dreaming about rain, but I saw that map in my dreams last night. Remember Barney's map? I saw it last night. I was right over it and swooped down to the place with the big tree, and I saw the pirates burying their treasure."

"Oh, Sandy, give me a break," shot back Peter. "That's lame. You dream because you have nothing better to do all night long. Waste of time. Look how stupid dreams are; I have dreams about a dump truck and a steam shovel. Both come right out of books my mom made me read over and over to learn how to read. So, of course, I have that dream every once in a while. It's just a dream. Dumb kid's stories and a dumb dream. Sometimes, I have a dream about Mike Mulligan and his steam shovel that can dig a whole basement in one day. Kid's a hero; the truck is a hero. Woo woo . . . So figure this out. How come I'm an old guy with gray hair and I'm still dreaming about kids' stories? It's just silly. It's day leftovers. You saw Barney's map, so you dream about it. Means squat. If Mom had made me do math flash cards, I'd be dreaming long division."

7

Sandy to the Top

"Hey, Ruth, if I needed to go somewhere, which jeep could I use?"

"Come on Sandy, go somewhere? Where? You take Peter's MacPorter to the dock. Take it now," she said gesturing toward the Frankenstein car that she had just serviced. "I just finished a tune-up and Mac needs a road test. Where ya' goin', Sandy?"

"I'm finished with all my work, and I thought I'd go up on the hilltop and see if I can find whatever that guy Barney is doing . . ."

"Ooohhhh. Gonna take a shovel with you?"

"Oh, shush. I was thinking that a shovel might be helpful if he needs just a few more shovel loads to get to the treasure."

"Be careful. It's nasty up there," Ruth chuckled. "And look!" Ruth laughed out loud, "Nicky is already in MacPorter with a trowel in his mouth. That dog knows what's up. Better take your flashlight. It'll be dark by the time you come home."

Sandy hopped in MacPorter and drove to the tool shed. He picked up a shovel and pick ax and then drove up the main road toward the mountain.

The road through the valley was a gentle grade before the big hill. As he climbed the hill, there were deep ruts where rain had washed away the surface exposing the solid rock under the road—and deep holes Sandy had to skirt around.

As the brush got thicker, MacPorter had to push bushes out of the way and struggle against brambles scraping the bottom. It was almost too thick to move. Just when it looked like it was getting impassable, Sandy saw that someone, maybe Barney, had cut the brush along the road to enable jeep travel—just barely.

After pushing through the worst of the brush, he popped out where the road was steep and open with low scrappy brush on the sides. Sandy had never been this high up on this island before. It was drier, not lush like the lowland tropical woods. To one side, he had a spectacular vista of the islands and bay below with the pale blue ocean, gentle waves, and ripples where the wind was working. On the other side was the steep hill up toward the mountaintop.

The road ended at the steepest part of the hill, where the person making the road had stopped. Barney's jeep was parked there and Sandy pulled MacPorter up next to it. He got out and called Barney's name as loud as he could. Over and over.

There was no answer. There was no sign of Barney anywhere. No tent, no camp, no pile of stuff. Despite the cut brush on the road and the parked jeep, It looked like no one had been here.

Sandy climbed between boulders and rock spires along a clear path to the top. He rounded the last big rock and crested the hill at the top of the path, and stepped onto a broad, mostly flat plain, the size of a ball field on top of the hill. The plain had a ring of stones and boulders along one edge and a stump—*REALLY* big stump—near the center. That must have been a very big tree. ok, so, big stump means big tree. That checks out. But ruins? Are there ruins anywhere?

All around him, Sandy saw lots of large and imposing boulders. There were piles of blocky-looking rocks around one edge of the broad flat plain. And as Sandy looked more intently, it was evident there were *several* piles of the blocky-looking rocks. Do they look like the ruins of something man-made or just piles of rocks?

Sandy walked to the center of the plain and stood on top of a *huge* stump. What did the map say? "Half from tree to ruins."

Sandy looked around. *Which* pile of rocks are the ruins? It could be any one of several different piles of big rocks. So, if there are a lot of places that could be ruins, then the halfway point could be so many places. And now that he stopped to notice, there were several large tree stumps.

That's when Sandy noticed that there were a *lot* of holes in the ground. It was clear that Barney had tried digging at many different places on the broad flat plain. Yet, there was no sign of him.

Sandy surveyed the big stump and the various piles of rocks. He picked one pile of blocky rocks that looked as if it had been *something*. He paced halfway from the stump to those rocks. Sure enough, at that spot, there was disturbed earth where Barney had evidently done some digging.

Fortunately, it was late afternoon when Sandy started, so he didn't have to spend a lot of time digging in futility. He worked hard at one spot while Nicky was darting around, digging a little here and digging a little there and having fun rolling in the loose dirt.

Finally, it was too dark to see. He kept at it until the batteries in Sandy's flashlight ran out, so he shrugged and gave up. "Come on Nicky. Let's go. This is futile." But the dog was too far away to hear Sandy.

Sandy called louder, "Nicky. Nick. Come on. Time to go home. There's no treasure here."

Nicky came running up to Sandy and sat, raised his paw, and dropped a stick at Sandy's feet.

"Ok, fella, just one throw," and Sandy hurled the stick not too far away. Nicky ran after it and played with the stick for a second, then came back to Sandy with the stick.

"Come on. We gotta go home. I said just one stick," but Sandy knew you can't throw away a stick that a dog is retrieving. The only way to stop Nicky was to make the stick disappear. It was yucky and slobbery, but Sandy slipped the stick into his pocket. Then, he turned and started trudging down the hill on the path back to MacPorter.

"Right here," said Sandy as he rounded the last big rock to where he'd left the cart. There was Barney's cart . . . but where was MacPorter?

Gone.

Sandy was flushed with panic. MacPorter had been here just a few minutes ago. ok, *hours* ago. *Barney's jeep is here but no MacPorter. Did someone come and steal it? Was Barney hiding? Did he take the cart? Or . . .* Sandy freaked and scrambled around in the pale starlight until he saw a hint of MacPorter's roof down the hill, over the edge, and in the gully below the road. He scrambled down to MacPorter. It had rolled down the hill and over the edge, bounced among the rocks, and came to rest on top of a big rock. It was too dark to see under the jeep to see if there was damage or dents.

Sandy climbed into the driver's seat and tried the engine. It made a horrible grinding noise. He tried again, and the grinding noise as worse. He tried Barney's jeep but that battery was dead.

"Oh, man. Now, I *am* in trouble." Sandy said to Nicky as he imagined how mad Peter was going to be that he wrecked MacPorter.

As they trudged slowly back down the road toward Sandell's Resort, Sandy stopped and looked at his hands, which were scraped and blistered from digging. "Look at your hands," Reed had said. "Take in where you are and what's happening. Press your hands together. Your hands trigger a moment of mindfulness. Take that moment to question your reality."

Sandy turned to Nick and said, "Thanks, Reed. My mind is full of here and now. And there's no question that this is real. It's like a nightmare; no Barney, no MacPorter, no treasure, no nothin.' But I am really sure that I am awake. No matter what Reed says about flying, I think we have to *walk* home. Let's go." Sandy lugged himself all the way back to the resort and flung himself into bed.

8

It Gets Worse—Way Worse . . .

When Sandy woke, his head was throbbing. It was late morning. He probably missed the morning meeting at Rhone's for breakfast and the day's agenda. Sandy leaped out of bed and rushed to Rhone's, knowing that Peter would be sitting by the bar, nursing his coffee, figuring out what needed to be done.

However, when Peter saw Sandy, he started to shout. "You cretin, Sandy. You nincompoop, you twit. How could you be such a profoundly stupid dope? You're the village idiot."

"Wait right dere," said Rhone. "We take turns bein' de village idiot. It ain' San'y's turn."

"Well, he *made* it his turn. Of all the bonehead things to do. Do you know what is NOT happening?" Peter yelled directly in Sandy's face. "You know what is NOT happening? Unit two plumbing is NOT leaking. I hate the leaks, but NOT leaking is worse. 'Not leaking' means we are OUT OF WATER! *You* are supposed to measure the water in the cistern every day. When did you tell me that the measurement was low and we needed to restrict water or buy water. When?"

"I'm so sorry, Peter. I forgot to measure the water. It just slipped my mind."

"Do you know what this means? The cistern is dry. No showers, no toilets, no hand washing, NO ICE . . ."

Several cries of agony came from voices at the stern end of the bar as the regulars figured out that NO ICE meant for their drinks.

Peter continued yelling, "You're such a nitwit and a dope . . ."

Rhone interrupted him, "Don't go all berserk on deh kid, Peter. He made a mistake. Jus' a mash up."

"Yeah, Peter," said Ruth from the stern end. "It's a simple mistake. You know the rules. We all get to make one mess per day. After that, you're borrowing from the future."

Rhone chuckled and shook his head, "I done so many mistakes, I must be borrowin' from decades yet to come. Besides, Peter, ain' you spozed to be supervisin' deh kid. Auntie always say 'All fish does bite, but de shark get di blame.' Youse in dis too and you heapin' alla blame on the kid, so don't go berserk."

"Berserk, I AM NOT GOING BERSERK!" Peter shrieked at the top of his voice, "I'm mad and I have a right to be mad," Peter fumed and ranted.

Sandy felt terrible inside. *Don't go berserk, Peter*, Sandy echoed in his mind. *I hope Peter calms down a little. The topic of MacPorter hasn't come up yet.*

Sandy looked down at his hands. The word *berserk* rolled over in his mind. Such an odd word. *Berserk.* What kind of . . .?

That's when Sandy snapped to full attention to right here and right now and thought, *Peter is all crazy-angry right now. Rhone is calming him down, and I'm looking at my hands.*

Pay attention to right here and right now. Sandy felt the piece of wood in his pocket, a reminder of the disaster last night. He pulled it out and put it on the counter.

Right now.
Tell him.
Be brave.
Bring it out.
Put it on the table.
Just like that.
Face it.
You made a mistake.
Rhone is saying it's ok.

Better to have Peter twice as mad now rather than telling him later and getting all riled up over MacPorter, all over again.

"Peter," Sandy started then hesitated. "I have some more bad news. I had a problem with MacPorter."

"Problem?" said Peter, in a calmer voice than a moment before. "What kind of problem?"

"Um, it's kinda, like, it rolled downhill and went over the edge of the road into a gully. I couldn't get it out. It's stuck up on something."

YOU WHAT?!" Peter shot up and leaned right into Sandy's face. "You did what?!"

"I, I, I . . ." Sandy stuttered and then blurted it all out, speaking very quickly. "I was up on the hilltop, and when I came back to where I parked MacPorter, it was gone. I think it rolled down the hill and into the gully. It might be fine, but it's stuck on something. It was so dark last night . . ."

Sandy trailed off as Peter interrupted. "YOU WRECKED MACPORTER?!?" Peter was back in a rage again. "You have got to be kidding. You wrecked MacPorter?! MY MacPorter?!? You let the water run out and you wrecked MacPorter . . ." Then, Peter stopped, and his shoulders relaxed, and he slumped slightly, then in a resigned whisper, he said, "It's just my day . . ."

"Take a chill pill, Peter," came the voice of Rhone, "Jes' re-lax. Bad news come in t'rees, and you only got two so far. One more comin'."

"Right. Right. Bad news in threes." Peter sat upright. His back straightened and stiffened. "I have more coming . . . But! I am Peter Sandell. I always get back up. Peter never quits. I get up. I never quit." Peter's rage dissolved into a look of steely determination.

Sandy was right. Adding more bad news to a pile of bad news didn't make Peter angrier. Rather, Peter seemed to give up and restart himself.

"Ok, ok," said Peter. "Let's figure out how we fix this mess. Where's Elroy?"

"He gone," Rhone said. "Deh havin' Saint Euplio festival on he island; he gotta go."

"Say that again. 'Eh OOP Leo? Who the hell is Eh Ooop Leo? How do you even say it?"

"Patron saint of good sailin'," said Rhone, "Very important on islan's. Auntie always say *'Breeze blow the pelican same place he wan' go.'* They gotta celebrate. An' Elroy gotta be there, he the gran' marshal of the parade."

"Yeah, yeah, I know. He has to go. I'm high and dry. Ug. Bad pun. Ok, ok . . . so, Ruth," he said turning to her, "we have to see if we can salvage dunderhead's MacWreck. Then, we need water. Rhone, you've done this before. Get on the phone with the water truck guy. We need a tank load of water, and call the barge captain. Set up a time to bring the truck over. Call . . . you know . . . call all the usual gang."

"Sure, Peter," said Rhone absentmindedly. He had picked up Sandy's piece of wood and was looking intently at it. For Rhone, something happened at that moment. He was looking *intently* at his hands holding a random piece of wood; or *was* it random? The rest of the beach disappeared for just a moment as Rhone realized he was holding something made of old smooth wood, with a *corner*. He was testing it with his fingers.

Meanwhile, Peter turned to Sandy. "Ok, bonehead. You probably set the brakes wrong. The question is, how badly dented and banged up is the jeep from hitting rocks on the way down. Broken axle . . . Punctured gas tank . . ."

Sandy wondered if he had done the brakes right? Had he pushed hard enough to set the brakes? Don't say anything.

"Ruth," Peter continued issuing orders, "We'll need your jeep and that winch. Spare parts and maybe a chain if we have to tow it back. The usual stuff."

"Aye, aye," she responded with a small salute and a smile. "I'm on it. Come up to my shop in about fifteen minutes. Everything is ready. I am always ready."

"Hey Peter," came the voice of Rhone in an inquisitive tone. "Look at dis piece ah wood. Dis ain' no tree stick." Rhone turned to Sandy and asked, "Where'd you git dis?"

"Nicky found it. Up on the top of the mountain where Barney's map said."

"Up the hilltop? Where dat guy's treasure map say?" Rhone asked, then turned to Peter, saying, "Look at this. It ol' smooth wood like hand rub. Look how de pieces fit together and de corner be roun'. This is no ordinary stick, Peter. Some body made dis. Maybe de corner of a box or a ches'."

With that, Peter came to see, muttering about how it could be trash too.

Rhone went on. "It mus' be part of something man-made that Nicky dug up . . ."

"Now, don't go out on some treasure-chest craziness," Peter said, "It's no surprise that there's junk wood from people-stuff up on that hill . . ." He paused, then added, "It *does* seem curious." He looked. He looked harder. He felt the smooth corner . . .

"We have to go get MacPorter out of the ditch, and we have to bring back Barney's jeep, so I suppose we could kick around a little up there and look around . . . Maybe now I want to see what the dog dug up. Or is this crazy?"

"Well," Sandy started, "I had a dream about that map and the mountain top. In Knight School, they said the things we dream of are windows to the real world. I bet there *is* treasure up there."

"Oh Lord, you were right, Rhone," said Peter. "Bad news comes in threes. First, no water; next, the MacWreck; and now Sandy wants his dreams to lead us to gold. Get over it, Sandy. Dreams are silly. Lemme tell you just how stupid dreams are.

"I had one a couple of weeks ago. Big burly guy with a big black beard, dressed up like Captain Morgan. A hook for a hand . . ."

Sandy blurted out, "Hey, that sounds like Captain Feit in my dreams."

"Fight or flight, he was just a big bad guy in my dream, and he was shouting at me, *'Pack my box with five dozen liquor jugs.'* Over and over. Like I couldn't miss that phrase. It's so dumb. See what I mean?"

Rhone whistled and added, "That soun' jus' like de pirates dem. Dey was always lookin' for rum. Bunch of crazed alkee-holics."

Ruth chuckled and then looked thoughtful. "Say that again, Peter. What was the guy yelling at you?"

Peter said it again, "*'Pack my box with five dozen liquor jugs.'* Over and over. The same dumb thing."

From the end of the bar came a voice. "I could drink to that. Ain' that sixty bottles of rum? That'd keep me busy for a day or two." There was laughter among the regulars at Rhone's Bar as they traded version of how long sixty bottles of booze would last them.

Meanwhile, Ruth had written it down and looked up from her note. "I wonder why he said five dozen instead of sixty? Oh, wait. It's the z. I see. There is q, j, x, and yup. He needed *dozen* for the Z. It's a pangram.

"A what?"

"Pangram. It's a sentence that has all the letters of the English alphabet in it at least once.

"See. The vowels are easy and so are most of the letters. Making a sensible sentence with the rare letters -- that's hard. See, box has an

X, and five has a V, and liquor has a Q. J is in jugs and Z is in dozen. This is a pangram."

"So, what's *that* mean?" asked a truly puzzled Peter.

"Oh, it doesn't mean anything, except that you and what you call stupid dreams just came up with a sentence that could be used to make a code."

"Are you telling me that I'm smarter than I think?"

"No, maybe just not as stupid as you think. That pirate phrase is kind of interesting" said Ruth, giving Peter a sly smile.

"That's nuts," said Peter. "Dismissed. All right folks. Let's go get bonehead's MacWreck. Time to act. Before you can do anything, you gotta get up, so let's go," said Peter as he got off his stool and they all headed toward Ruth's.

C03 ✪ 80

Everyone agreed that Ruth's creation of MacPorter was a work of art, but her own jeep was even more extraordinary. She had welded together parts and pieces that made her jeep a perfect fit for her interests.

"I call her *Electra* because she has the juice. The roof is a set of solar panels," said Ruth when she had taken Sandy on a tour of her jeep once. "The solar panels feed this bank of batteries here under the truck bed." She pressed a button and a hydraulic lift raised the truck bed to expose her arrangement of the sub-floor area. "The batteries feed my whole DC electric system that runs the inverter that turns DC to AC to run the flood lights on these extensible poles and the welding system and the air compressor. All the tools run off the air compressor like that jackhammer and the lift-jack. I can lift over twelve tons with the lift-jack alone and the winch is rated to pull a tractor-trailer truck." There were custom-made metal boxes on the sides with Ruth's collection of tools. They were all good tools, but her powerful winch, on the front of the jeep was what Peter wanted.

When Peter got to the shop, they all packed into her jeep and took off for the top of the hill. Nicky was sitting with Sandy in the back,

76

Peter up front and Ruth driving. For Sandy, it was *déjà vu*—same ruts, same brambles, same squeeze. They popped out near the top of the hill on the open road, past the gully with MacPorter perched on the rock and then the end of the road and Barney's jeep.

They all walked up the path between boulders and rock spires until they came out at the large plain on the hilltop. They called out Barney's name over and over until Sandy said, "If he's here, he's not answering."

They wandered around in silence, first taking in the big stump in the middle of the plain and then all the holes and starts of holes that pockmarked the hilltop. Barney must have spent a long time trying different holes.

Peter broke the silence, saying, "Sandy's right; there's no Barney here. If he fell down a ravine, then he's buzzard food by now. Let's see if we can find which hole is where the dog dug up that wood." They all looked around with no idea where the spot might be, and then they all looked at Nicky as if he would show them. Nicky had no idea. He was anxious and embarrassed with everyone staring at him, so he did sit-and-paw.

"Hold on, guys," said Peter. "The dog isn't going to show us anything as long as we're paying attention to him. We have to stop looking at him."

So, they all pretended not to be interested in Nicky. The dog still didn't get it. Sit-and-paw.

"ok, so let's all ignore Nicky," said Ruth. "If we all go do something else, then he might go find his spot and dig again."

Peter turned and walked toward the edge of the flat plain to investigate the blocky rocks. Ruth went back down to look at MacPorter, and Sandy went to the other end of the plain to investigate a really large rock he had noticed before. They left Nicky alone.

Peter soon realized that there were *lots of rocks* and lots of piles of blocky rocks and some of those piles might have once been something. He saw how hard it was to pick where to start to go "half from tree to ruins." Too many choices of what might be *ruins*. No wonder Barney had so many false starts.

Ruth was checking on MacPorter. No big damage. Just sitting on a rock with its wheels off the ground. It had just a few dents. Not a big deal. A couple of days for repairs.

Meanwhile, Sandy found odd lines carved in the big rock at the far end of the flat plain on the hilltop. Weird. Kind of like the lines on Barney's map.

That's when Nicky barked.

They all came running. Nicky was over a hole and another scrap of wood was sticking up out of the dirt. The corner of a chest was exposed. They dove in, all at once, all hands digging. Their scrambling hands and shovels worked furiously to expose the wooden chest. Once the sides were in sight, it was easy to put a shovel under the chest and pry it out. "That's weird," said Peter, "there's loose earth around this box." Then they pried the top open.

One must stop here to consider this moment.

Imagine you are extracting a buried chest from under the earth.

Consider the situation.

Someone wanted to hide this.

Something valuable or important is in here.

You found it. You are about to open the unknown.

Coins or gems, books, or wet rotten paper or what?

The unknown. Unearthed. Revealed.

Pure exhilaration.

Look at your hands, Sandy.

Be here now.

Lid up!

Nothing

Nothing?

"Well there is a rolled-up piece of leather," said Sandy as he picked it up. "This looks like the map Barney had." As Sandy unrolled the piece of leather, a single gold coin fell out. He picked it up; and yelled, "A gold doubloon! Old gold! Real treasure!"

Peter snatched the coin from Sandy's hand saying, "That will just pay for fixing MacPorter."

Then Ruth snatched the coin from Peter saying, "Since I will do the repair work, this should be just about enough to pay for parts and labor." She pocketed the coin.

"Hey guys, look at this. Rolled up inside the map is a note. It's from Barney Elmer."

"Read it," said Peter and Ruth at once.

Sandy read, "I took the treasure and left. Sorry about the jeep. Here's a coin for whatever I owe. Next time, trust your instincts. Barney Elmer." They examined the chest, and sure enough, the imprint of coins on the bottom and sides made it clear the box had held a lot of coins.

"Real treasure," said Peter.

Then silence; then muttering, all muttered thoughts under their breath.

"He musta been right . . ."

"There really was treasure . . ."

"What if we had helped . . ."

We could'a dug some . . ."

"We were so close . . ."

They walked slowly down the hill to Barney's jeep, but there was no spark in their step, just sullen sadness. They worked together with Ruth's winch to pull MacPorter out of the gully, and Ruth fiddled with stuff and got it running. After jumpstarting Barney's jeep, there were three jeeps, so Peter, Ruth and Sandy each drove home alone. Alone with their thoughts. The same thoughts.

How come I didn't help?

What was I doing that was so important?

Why didn't I see that his map was real?

And the one line none of them could bear to say out loud: *I could have been rich.*

That night at Rhone's was somber and sad.

Even Rhone was dejected. "You mean, when we was small fry, we was playin' on top of a treasure chest . . ."

No one could quite say, "We blew it."

9

Fly Somewhere—Somewhere Worth Going

Sandy felt the crisp air surge into his lungs, bringing with it the smell of flowers. Sandy knew this place. It was the canyon with the Knight School cabin. *There must be a path*, he thought. *Find the path. Look for the sign. There's always a sign. Whoops! That was Nicky running by. He brushed by me. He touched me.* Suddenly, Sandy was hovering. Not flying but *hovering*. Gliding along the path.

Wait! Sandy stopped. There was something new. The sound of waterfalls. He looked around. *This canyon has always seemed to be just dry ragged rock; spires and boulders*, he mused. *How come I never noticed any waterfalls? I never heard the sound of water hurtling over cliffs and crashing onto the rock below. The air is so full of cool moisture; that's new.*

He looked up from his reverie and found himself standing at the edge of the porch of the Knight School cabin.

"Hey, it's Sandy," said one of the kids in the circle as Sandy stepped up and settled into a chair on the broad board porch of the Knight School.

"Are there always waterfalls here?" Sandy asked. "I never saw them or heard them before."

"Wow, you're *just* hearing them now?" chuckled Mars in a self-righteous way. "They've always been here. At least since *I* noticed them."

"Well, maybe for you," tossed back Blake. "I think they only appear when your senses become more alert and aware during dream time."

"Yeah," added Kat, "I didn't hear them until around the time I started to dream in color."

"It's weird," said Sandy, "Like I am hearing and seeing what is right here that I never saw or heard before."

That makes me wonder what else is right in front of me that I don't see? Ya know, like how stupid am I?"

"I don't think we see most things until we name them," offered Grace. "Like when we open up more, we can discover what was right here all the time. But Sandy, you look troubled," she continued. "What happened?"

They were all expecting to hear Sandy talk about flying dreams but instead Sandy started to explain the series of disasters that had happened to him—wrecking MacPorter, the long walk home, being yelled at by Peter about water . . . Sandy was almost crying as he described Peter making fun of him for talking about a dream. In the end, Sandy was muttering about an empty treasure box, saying, "I could have had some treasure. I can't believe how much I messed up this week."

"Whoa," said Mars. "Like no one ever made a mistake before. I mess up every day. It's ok."

"Sandy seems to have had a particular run of bad luck," said Kat.

"Yeah, you sure had a worse week than me," said Blake. "I just did normal things."

Grace opened her eyes slowly, then wide, saying, "Sandy is miserable and needs help. Maybe we can give him some."

"So, what do we do, Grace?" asked Blake. "Where's Reed?"

"He's with some other dreamers now," she said, "but we can do work ourselves. We always explore alternatives in dreams. What are some of Sandy's alternatives?"

Blake was ready. "You mean, like, what would you do if you made a mistake at work or broke something important?"

"Yea, that's it," said Grace. "What else could someone do?"

"I'd apologize to the owner and ask for forgiveness," said Kat.

"Make amends," added Blake. "Do what needs to be done until it's right."

Mars had an idea, "Find *treasure* to pay for it."

"I wonder what I'd do if I found an empty treasure box?" mused Blake.

Mars flung back, "Fill it up with dream gold coins."

And Blake added, "I'd look for another one. If there's one, who knows how many more . . ."

Grace had a different take on the chest. "I'd treat the chest like it's a treasure all by itself and be pleased to own it—empty or not."

Kat interrupted. "Maybe you find the treasure *in you*. What's in your treasure chest? What treasure are you putting in your chest?"

"In my chest?" responded Sandy. "Like valuables?"

"Well, Sandy, *chest* isn't only a treasure chest,' said Kat. "your chest is where your heart is. What's in your *heart*?"

Mars was right on it. "What she said. What do you hold in your heart? Love for others? What's Reed always say, 'It's from your heart that all dream connections arise.'"

Kat jumped right back, "I think this is about all the valuable treasure that isn't gold. All the treasure your dreams have brought."

"Hey, I have an idea," said Blake, sitting up and fully alert. "What if we gave our dreams over to Sandy tonight? We all have times we messed up and felt miserable like Sandy. What if we work on having a dream with something from our life that will speak to Sandy."

"Sure," said Grace, "Who's willing to bring Sandy into your heart and reach out to him in your dreams?"

"That's cool, Grace," said Kat. "Like, give my dreams over to Sandy tonight?"

"I suppose you could say it that way." Grace responded, "If you hold Sandy in your heart, then you'll find something in your life and in your dreams that touches on his situation? Who's in?"

Blake was ready. "I'm in, I'll let you use a night's worth of my dreams. No rent."

Kat agreed. "I'm in, too. I'll let you use some of my dream time."

"Me too," said Mars, flexing his arms. "I'm tough. Maybe I can chase some monster away with you."

At that, and because this was a magical place called Knight School, a poster appeared right then on the wall and they all read it out loud.

"I promise to remember a dream for you tonight. I will reach out with a full heart and meet you in dream space and help you in my dreams. I have my paper and pencil by my bed. I will write when I wake. I will think of you as I fall asleep."

"That's cool," said Sandy. "I guess that poster is like the waterfalls; it didn't need to be there until we were ready to try this. Then, just what you need is right in front of you."

"Ok, guys, let's go," said Blake like a quarterback. "As we go to sleep, let's re-up our intention to help Sandy. Imagine your heart connecting with his heart, meeting in dream space. When you finish dreaming, come back to Knight School and see what we discover."

With that, they all reached out on either side and touched the hand of the person beside them. When they made a complete circle, they leaned back, closed their eyes, and listened to the sound of everyone humming the same drone sound as they returned to their own dreams.

ೞ ✪ ೞ

Blink. Blink. Awake. Or am I?
No! Still dreaming.

Sandy was on the deck of the pirate ship with the dog. Same plank, same pirates all around him, but no swords or weapons; they were laughing at him.

Captain Feit offered hearty belly laughter and said, "Hahahahaha. Hell's bells, kid. You found one and you quit. That's the funniest thing ever. You can't quit. We buried twenty chests of loot up on that hilltop, and you're are all done after one." They all roared with laughter. "Hahahahaha."

Bonny Anne was the only one who seemed to lament Sandy's feeling of loss. "He says twenty; there may be more. Dig deeper, lad."

"Deeper?" asked Sandy as he stood, yet again, on the pirate's plank. "Deeper into what? Deeper into history? Deeper into words? Deeper into me? Deeper where?"

With that thought, Sandy took Nicky's paw in his hand, and they rose up and shot straight up in the air, far above the pirate ship and into clouds. Sandy was looking down with Nicky by his side. For a few minutes, they just hovered high above the ship and marveled at their flight. *Go somewhere useful*, thought Sandy. *Bring home treasure.*

Sandy aimed himself at the island's mountain peak and soared through the clouds, tasting the water of the clouds as he flew down and landed on top of the hill on Water Island.

Sandy landed on the broad flat plain. It was just the same . . . yet different. There was a large stone tower at one edge and a very small tree in the center.

Sandy turned and looked down into the bay. There was a ship but not a pirate ship. It was a much older ship. A Viking ship like a long sea-going canoe with one big sail and oars. A *lot* of oars. And it's on the rocks . . . Not going any—"

Then, a voice behind Sandy said, "Like thou our ship? Vee call it *Langskip*. Can you fix it?"

Sandy turned, and right behind him was a huge block of a man, and right behind *him* was a strikingly tall person with a metal helmet. Farther away at the base of the stone tower, there was a small group of heavy-set, stumpy men.

"Yikes!" Sandy stammered as he fell back. "Who are you?"

I'm Rundwulf. This be Whorf," he said pointing to the tall person with the helmet. "I the captain. They the brains."

"You don't look like pirates. Who are you?" said Sandy, peering around to give the gang a long look.

"We're not pirates, though some say anyone doing a Viking raid is a pirate," said the tall person with the metal helmet.

Sandy said, "Well, sir, *you* look like a Viking. The others . . . not so much." With that, he looked over the gang wearing T-shirts and shorts like they were on a trip to the beach.

"Captain," said Whorf, "they be puzzled. The boy doesn't believe vee be Vikings."

"Aye," said Rundwulf. "They all want oss to *look* like Vikings. Stupid be it." That said, Rundwulf turned and addressed the group of men by the tower. "All right, ya jolly rugged gang, put on yer berserks and head kettles. The ones with the horns."

"But Rundwulf," came the whiny voice of one of the men, "It's too hot for bearskin shirts."

"Aye, just do it," said Rundwulf, "Vee have to costume up like the boy thinks vee *should* look. They will not believe oss if vee don't look right."

Upon hearing these words, the men opened their rucksacks and pulled out bearskin shirts and iron helmets with horns attached to the sides.

"Rundwulf!" came the voice of another in the gang, "These horns are daft. None of oss ever wore this. Vee be dressing like a picture book."

"Just do it," said Rundwulf.

"Well, now you look better," said Sandy as the men were all in their garb, "At least now you *look* like Vikings. Are you really Vikings?"

"Vee be North'men," said Rundwulf, "but thou can call oss Vikings if thou like. Thy people mangled our word, *viking*. When vee work, det is *viking*; a raiding party, an invasion for pillage and plunder. It's seasonal work. Raid in summer, forth and back, then home in winter to tell sagas of conquests during beer-drinking contests. Det is what North'men do.

"Vee settled the whole north world from the Volga in Rus in the east to the Orkneys, Faroes, Iceland, Greenland, Vinland, and beyond," Rundwulf continued. "Vee never stopped. Among explorers thee only hear of the ones who come back. Vee got this far and stayed."

Whorf added, "This little band be what thou call explorers; the leading edge. Tip of the sverd—sword to thee. Vee be the first-in raiders, and kick up rumpus. Nothing stops oss."

"But why are you here?" asked Sandy.

"Home was Iceland," started Rundwulf, "but vee be wanderers. Vee took one of the langskips and set out to explore—to boldly go where no North'men had ever gone before.

"Vee roamed down the coast of thy 'new' world and just kept going. Vee got to these sunny islands and decided to stay. Now vee be more like *retired* Vikings."

"But why are you here?" asked Sandy, puzzled.

"But the real reason?" Rundwulf answered, "Vee fetched up here when our langskip struck rocks. Vee had a shipwright builder with oss, but her went to Valhalla. Vee be stuck. All North'men know. *Some go to and never come fro.* That is oss.

"I see that's why you're on this island," Sandy mused, *"But why are you in my dream?"*

"Oh that," said Rundwulf, who turned to Whorf saying, "Whorf, thou be the brains and linguist. Explain thou thus to them."

Whorf sat down on a convenient rock, pulled off the steel kettle helmet and released long flowing blond hair.

91

"You're a woman!" Sandy sputtered.

"What were you expecting?"

"Well," Sandy paused, not sure how to answer, "Rundwulf did say *North'men*. I just assumed . . ."

"Oh that. The damn men write all the history. Of course, the men call all of oss North'MEN. When vee invented the word *men,* vee meant all people, not just the ones who don't make babies. But the men put their name on everything. North'MAN invasion. Vee created all people being equal and invented words like "they" and "them." Vee have nothing about men or women being better or worse. But men mark everything like dogs pee on trees. Gotta mark men's turf. Men . . ."

"But in a raiding party . . .?" Sandy was incredulous.

"Of course, thou cannot imagine women in a raiding party. Men think *they're* the only fighters. *Women are more fierce than men.* Besides, women make men; men don't make anything; that's why men raid and steal. They have to prove their prowess to themselves.

"But not me. I be one of the few who can calm a berserker. That is a sign of holiness. I have that holiness. My touch brings peace . . ."

As she trailed off, she pulled out a clay pipe, lit it from a glowing ember that she unwrapped from her pouch, and drew on the smoke.

"Thou used our word. That summoned oss. When thou use our words, thou use our thoughts and, in that instant, vee are alive in thee."

"What did I say to summon you?"

"Berserk," shot back Rundwulf. "That word is of oss."

"Right," explained Whorf, drawing on her pipe. "Berserk is the bear skin shirt vee wear. Bear Shirt . . . Berzerk. Vee put on bearskin shirts when vee go raiding. Thou would say vee are going *berserk*. Great word. *Our* word."

Sandy asked, "But why are your words in my head?

"Of course, our words are in thy head," said Rundwulf. "Thy English is full of North words."

"Like what?" asked Sandy.

93

"*Slaughter* is from oss," Rundwulf said proudly, then added, "*ransack, anger, hel* . . . All words from oss in thy language."

"*Slaughter? Ransack?*" Sandy stammered. "Those aren't nice words. Did you make all our bad words?"

"Oh, no," continued Whorf as she cleaned her pipe. "Vee gave thee pretty ones, too. *Gift* is our word. Thy *thank* comes from oss. Some of thy nicest thoughts come from oss. *Far Vel* is a gift from our language. Far Vel, fare thee well."

With this, Whorf leaned back and recited a verse with the gang chiming in for the last part of each line.

> *Thou can't thrive or die—without our words*
> *Thou can't be happy or jolly—without our words*
> *Can't be wrong or weak or work—without our words*
> *No blunder, plunder, or cast asunder—without our words*
> *No bread to bake nor cake to eat—without our words*
> *No give and take, nor to and fro—without our words*
> *No dirt, nor dregs, nor bitch, nor birth—without our words*
>
> *Elves, trolls, giants, dwarves—They are all our words.*
> *Their, thee, they and them—all our words*
> *Every gift is ours, every thanks as well—all our words*
> *And when parting, say Far Vel.*

The gang of Vikings all applauded as Whorf finished, and then she added, "And when thou dream at night; that word, *dream*, is our word too. When thou use our words thou think our thoughts and vee are alive in thee."

Sandy was wondering how many ideas in his head had roots in these old words.

"So, are your words on that pirate map?" he asked.

"Aye son, thou saw our runes on the pirate's map. That triggered oss. The pirate who made thy map used our runes like a code. But there is more. Deeper still is our riddle. Now, thou figure it out.

"What time am I?
When your moon shadow kisses the sunrise
The black ocean sparkles silver
The sea swallows, the moon lies
Eastern sky turns scarlet, then starless.
What time am I?"

"Am I supposed to know what time it is?" Sandy choked. "I have no idea . . . Let me see, sounds a little like sunrise."

"Ah, it does sound like sunrise," responded Whorf. "But not just any sunrise. It's specific, Sandy. When can your moon shadow kiss the sunrise. *Your* moon shadow."

"Moon shadow?" Sandy mused, "I never saw a moon shadow before I came here. I only see my moon shadow under the full moon."

"So, when can a moon shadow kiss sunrise?" continued the probing Whorf.

Sandy mulled this over until Rundwulf let out a sigh and barked out, "It's the full moon set, Sandy. Thou land people never see thus. Ah, but across the ocean, from the deck of a ship or high on an island, it's like sunset but the moon sparkles silver and pale blue on the sea at full moon set . . ." He trailed off.

Whorf picked up as Rundwulf got lost in thought saying, ". . . end of night, coming of dawn, The moon is setting . . . the sun is rising . . . both at once . . . opposites . . . Something new always happens when the full moon sets. New day. New month. Something new."

As she finished, Rundwulf snapped out of his reverie and spoke straight into Sandy's face, saying, "Vee North'men were here ages ago. Vee built the tower that fell to ruins. Vee planted the tree. Vee carved our runes in one big stone. Now! Thou! Find the rune stone."

And Whorf added, "Vee come from deep within thee, Sandy . . . Find us. Far Vel."

Nicky's paw tapped at the side of Sandy's leg. The dog started to rise.

"Dog's right. Gotta go," said Sandy as he put his hand around Nicky's paw, and they flew off high above the islands and into dream space.

10

Come on, Peter, We Gotta Go Back

In Peter's cottage, he was asleep and dreaming. He found himself with Piper. They were on the beach, running where the wet sand was compact. Full streaming sunshine. Running with the wind, her hair blowing in the wind. The smile. The radiance. Then, back in the cottage. She was opening her jewelry box. She was holding the jewelry box Peter bought her when they got engaged. She had all her rings and bracelets—all her jewels in the treasure chest. Such a simple yet elegant jewelry box. But, what was she holding now? She had a second jewelry box. It was just like his gift, but different—maybe newer; maybe larger. The shape was like a heart. It was shimmering like it had light inside. She opened the lid, and the glint of sunlight coming through Peter's window woke him just at that moment.

A dream, thought Peter. *A dream with Piper. She was lovely. The jewelry boxes. Why did she have a second jewelry box?*

A wave of sadness swept over Peter, who was feeling the loss of Piper. "I just want to go back to bed and stop all of this."

Then, he sat up, straightened his back, and put a resolute look on his face. "You're only defeated when you quit, and I *never* quit."

ℭℜ ✪ ℬ

The sound of the waterfalls is louder this morning, thought Reed as he moved around the building, checking on the students in his charge.

On the porch, there were the kids who came for Knight School and were part of Sandy's circle. On the inside were more rooms and more groups of sleepers, each group clustered together. Dreamers were sprawled in the living room, among sofas and chairs, on thick mats on the floor. Some were snoring. Some were curled up. Others needed their bed covers tucked back in.

Reed moved like a nurse among patients, checking, monitoring for movement behind their eyelids, and when one of the dreamers was having a particularly difficult nightmare, Reed would stand nearby and offer his dream spirit into their dream to help.

As they woke, Reed had warm drinks and paper on which to draw and write dream memories. A sign appeared on the wall that said, "Draw a note, write a picture, bring something back from the dream world."

As Sandy's friends awoke, Reed came and sat with them as they shared their dreams, ideas, and stories.

Mars went first, "I had this zany dream . . ."

Grace interrupted. "Remember to tell a dream like you are in it right here and now."

"Oh yeah, continued Mars. "I'm driving a huge tank over a bridge to an island. Not an army tank but a huge tank truck. I'm taking water to a place like a light house. I have to put the water in the basement. It's deep and dark and the water makes a splashing noise as it falls."

Blake was next. "I'm wearing a round flat-top hat. I work in a hotel. I haul luggage to people's rooms. I'm taking a plate of big hamburgers up to a hotel room, but the elevator will only go down."

"Sounds like you're a porter. A hamburger porter. Ha!" said Mars with a laugh.

"No, it's better than that," said Sandy, jumping in. "Blake had a Big Mac Porter in his dream. Just like my jeep, MacPorter!"

"Well, I did carry a lot of things for my family this week in *WakeWorld*, so maybe that's the porter part," said Blake, "But the elevator going down—that's for Sandy."

"That's so weird," said Kat, "I was going down too. Walking down stairs, then climbing down ladders to a deeper level. In a small room, there is a tiny door in the wall. I have to get down on my hands and knees to see into the door. I lie down and crawl forward, farther and farther into the tunnel. It's a tight fit. I have to shimmy along the smooth floor, always with light up ahead."

"That sounds like a classic rebirth dream to me," said Grace, "We've *all* had the experience of being born. It's universal and must be a very deep memory. There are no words for memories that deep. Maybe Kat is going through some daytime changes that are like being born."

"Oh, now I see," said Kat with a vacant look. "My family just moved into a new house—a new school. No one knows me. I guess that's a lot like being reborn into a new me."

"Yeah, I see," answered Blake. "When you move to a new place, you get to rethink everything about who you are and how you want to be known. It's like a renewal."

"That's right," added Grace. "Perfect time to change your nickname or pronouns. New school. New you. That's in-*sight*"

Then, it was Sandy's turn to share his dream, though he was a little reluctant about sharing how Peter had teased him for dream-sharing. He told them all about the Vikings and all the funny words like *wer* and *oss* and *thee* and *thou* . . . and *far vel* and how Whorf said they were deep within him.

"I'm not sure I want a bunch of Vikings loose inside me?" asked Mars. "I wonder if they mean they are inside literally . . ."

"Maybe, Mars, but I don't think dreams are ever literal. They always allude to something else, like everything is something else, even sometimes sideways related." said Kat. "What part of Sandy is trying to speak with those odd words?"

"Yeah," said Blake. "I think the dream is telling Sandy that the secret to the treasure is deep in those odd words."

They were quiet, and Reed gathered them back to the topic, "What's the common theme in all of your dreams?"

Blake had it first, "Mars is hauling water and putting it into a deep underground tank. In my own dream, I'm a Big Mac Porter, and my elevator is going down. Kat is deep in the earth and Sandy has Vikings deep inside. Oops, I think I'm in over my head . . ." They all laughed.

"What Blake is saying is that all of our dreams have something going down deeper. But deeper into what?"

Kat had it, "Deeper in yourself. Sandy, what treasure is down deep inside you?"

Blink. Blink. Awake.

℘ ✪ ℘

Back in his bed. Back at Sandell's Resort, Water Island. Comfy safe bed.

Sandy lay in bed. *Not quite time for Morning Meeting. Dig deeper. With a shovel? What if I dug deeper with a shovel? But where? I need to know where to dig deeper . . .*

But wait. What is Reed always saying. It's all metaphors. Something is a picture of something else. Dig deeper may not be with a shovel, but it

99

might be. Maybe we need to dig that hole deeper and there is more below. Or does it mean to dig deeper into what is right in front of me?

Sandy stretched and got up. He changed from bed shorts to work shorts, put on his T-shirt and sandals and was up and out on the way to Rhone's Reef to see what Peter was doing.

Peter was staring at the beach, sitting at his spot at Rhone's. Looking at the flow of people across the beach—at women in bathing suits . . . young women with long flowing hair waving gently in the wind. Peter was lost in thought.

Rhone poked Peter, saying, "Yo, Peter, wha's gine on? You been staring at de same dame fo' a long time. Yo, Peter, snap outta dis."

Peter shook his head, sat up, and took a long drink of his cold soda as Sandy came up to Rhone's.

"Peter, I want to go back," said Sandy, "I think there's more."

"We did that, Sandy," said Peter. "Remember? Empty box."

"But I know there must be something more up there."

Rhone said, "It do seem strange der would be only ONE box ah treasure. I been thinkin' 'bout dat too. What if dat Barney guy missed de real loot?"

"I think there's more treasure," said Sandy. **"I'd rather try and be wrong than never know."**

Peter snapped to attention and sat straight up, "Why do you think . . . How do you know?"

"I know you think this is crazy," said Sandy, "but I had this dream with the pirates who buried the treasure. They said that there's more treasure on that mountain top. They laughed at me."

"Now you getting' it from boff sides," laughed Rhone. "Peter's laughin' at ya, and dem dream pirates, laughin' at you too. Auntie always say, 'The higher the monkey climb, the more he tail show.' You makin' youself uh easy target."

Peter stopped laughing. "But why do you believe that people talk to you in your dreams? That's just silly."

"No, Peter. You wrong," Rhone spoke sharply. "Dreams is deep. 'Mong my people, dreams is omens and porten's. They tell what's comin'. Kind'a like a doctor's shot, we dream stuff 'at might happen so we ready when it does. An' dreams is where the *other world* speak to us. You know, de jumbies dem."

"Other world? Jumbies?" Peter raised an eyebrow as his voice trailed off.

"Come on, Peter," said Rhone, "Don't knock Sandy and he dream. He might be right."

Might be right, Peter mused.

Might be right, thought Sandy. Emboldened by this idea he jumped in like a fighter ready to strike.

"Yeah, Peter. What if dreams are tapping into something deep, like deep memory from when you were a baby—maybe from earlier generations? Maybe we have residue from all of history in us. Maybe we can remember being cave people if we needed to. Like our cave mind is still deep in there. So, I had Vikings in my dreams and pirates too. They said there's more treasure. Dig deeper."

"Vikings . . . Pirates . . . Are you nuts?" Peter was ranting. "Sandy how many times do I have to tell you that dreams are stu—"

His voice trailed off as he whispered. "Wait, I had a dream last night. I remember one. What was in my dream . . ." his voice trailed off again. "Hold it. I can remember." Peter stared off into space as he drifted along with this thought while Sandy told Rhone about the Pirates and Vikings.

"That's pretty weird, Sandy," said Rhone. "Pirates I can see. Dey was really here. But Vikings . . .? Das over de top fo' me. Das bazzady."

"What's bazz-a-day?" Sandy asked.

"Auntie used dat for anyone talkin' crazy. Talkin' 'bout Vikings on this island? Das bazzady."

Peter came back from being lost in his thoughts. "ok, ok, so this is weird, you guys, but I actually remember a dream from last night."

"Flash cards and kid's books ag'in?" asked Rhone.

"No, I was with Piper," Peter started. "She was so lovely. She had a jewelry chest. She had the one I gave her but she had a second one too.

It was shaped like a valentine. It had like a light inside . . . a light inside a second treasure chest."

Peter's eyes had the faraway look of a man digesting a new idea. Exploring what might be and having to grapple with the idea that his dream could be telling him something that he might be missing—something sitting right in front of him. What if Piper was telling him there are more treasure chests? Two jewelry chests. *What if . . .? What if I've been wrong?*

He drifted in mind space for just a moment, then snapped to attention and turned to Sandy and said, "Come on, Sandy. We have to go back . . . There *is* more up there."

11

Where Do We Dig?

Peter and Sandy took MacPorter back up the mountain. Peter was talking out loud to himself about what they should do. "Dig deeper where we found one chest. The second one must be under the first one. We should dig deeper where we found that. Deeper. Or wait, what if the second chest is just to one side of the first one. That would mean we need to dig a ring around where we found that one. Out about chest width. But what if it's further out? This is insane, you know, Sandy. This is insane. We're chasing something we saw in a dream. Chasing non-existent gold. And when we stop, we will always have the nagging feeling that if we had just dug one little bit more. This is a classic bottomless pit. No matter whe—"

Sandy interrupted, "Yeah, but you saw two jewelry chests, and my pirates said there was more."

After that, they rode along in silence.

As they got to the top of the hill and parked the jeep, they walked up the last bit of path to the top of the mountain.

"Ok, so let's go over where we found the first chest and just go down until we hit the second chest," said Peter. With that, they both took shovels and began digging deeper under where they found Barney's chest.

They managed to do that for a couple of hours until they were three chests deep into the dirt with nothing to show for it.

"Ok, said Peter. Ok, maybe we're digging in the wrong place."

Sandy agreed. "Like you said, what if the second chest is beside where the first one was?"

Peter wiped his very sweaty and dirty brow and nodded in agreement. "Then, we need to dig over here and there and then keep moving around," he said, pointing to opposite sides of the hole they had dug.

So they each took a side and dug to the side, and slowly worked their way around the perimeter of their hole until they had expanded their search out to a much wider circle. Still nothing but rocks and dirt. And in most places, they hit solid rock about six feet down.

Hours and hours passed.

"Hold up here, Sandy," said Peter. "I hit solid rock here, again. This whole plain is a layer of dirt sitting on top of a solid rock base. No matter where I dig, I keep hitting something solid."

"Maybe that's why there are so many places where Barney started a hole. Maybe he hit rock bottom on all of them."

". . . Except the one with the loot."

"Let's take a snack break, Sandy. This is work," said Peter, and he plopped down beside the hole they had dug. They rested for a while, catching their breath and taking in the scene.

"Rhone packed some food for us. Here's your pack," said Peter, handing Sandy a package from Rhone's snack bag. Then, a few seconds later: "What'd ya get?"

"Ugh," exclaimed Sandy, "Leftovers from Ka'nibal's Feast night. Elbow macaroni with head cheese. I hate head cheese."

Peter looked up from his bag, saying, "I got baby back ribs. Not good with my teeth. Wanna swap?"

"Wow, sure," said Sandy as they exchanged bags. "I love his ribs. Here, you get the mac and cheese. Soft food, you ol' softie . . ."

"Way excellent swap, Sandy. We're a good team. Jack Sprat and all that." Then, after a pause, Peter continued, "You know, Sandy, I'm really sorry for how I yelled at you the other day. I was being a big bully, and that's not what I meant at all."

"Ah, I'm ok with it," said Sandy. "I get bullied a lot. Being here, I had almost forgotten Moe Lesko and his gang. They were always mean to me. The shrimpy kid takes a lot of bullying."

"I know about bullies. I was the fat kid in my school," said Peter. "*Fat, dumb and stupid.*' I heard that taunt every day. I might have been chubby and unathletic but I was never dumb or stupid, so that really hurt. I had a big-muscle bully who tormented me. All brawn, no brains. He took my lunch money. He'd kick up a scuffle just to get me to trip and fall so he could rub my face in the dirt."

"You too? Taking my lunch money. That's from the same playbook as what I got." said Sandy. "And the scuffle after school just to trip me and rub my face in the dirt. Your guy sounds just like my guy; big brawny dope who gets joy from tormenting easy target kids. The skinny kid gets picked on by kids who aren't even the big bullies."

"I know." said Peter with a sigh. "skinny or fat, you aren't in the cool kids' group, so they pick on all us outliers. Always getting dirt in my face from some big kid and his three big oaf buddies. I got the shit kicked out of me too many times . . . Made me like leather on the outside. Gotta keep the walls up. That's how I managed.

"I used to love my books," Peter continued, "and my bully was always yanking them out of my hand. Musta happened to me a hundred times. I'm sitting somewhere reading a story, and the big bully guy comes up with his two goons, yanks the book out of my hands, rips out the next few pages, and tears them up. I hated that kid."

"No way," Sandy said perking up. "Your bully took your book and ripped pages out. Mine too. I really hated that. The worst was when I was really young and a bully took my Teddy bear and hung him up in the jungle gym in the park. Too high for me to climb. I had to get grown-ups to rescue my bear."

Peter asked "You had a bear? I had a bear too. He was my best friend until I met Piper. My bear never said anything bad about me, never called me names, never an unkind word. My bear is still the only one I can count on to always be there for me.

"Yeah, that's like my bear." added Sandy, "Do you still have your bear."

Well… This may sound silly from a middle age man," said Peter looking down at the ground. "but, yeah, I still have my bear. He is on my bureau. I see him every day. Still there. Yes, and I still talk to him too. Such a good listener."

"Hey Sandy," Peter sat upright and turned to face Sandy, "If anyone anywhere ever bullies you again, you just stand up for yourself, be better than them."

"Hummm," Sandy mused. "Doesn't sound easy."

"Yo, Sandy," Peter continued "That kid who bullied me in school—you know what happened to him? That kid died in a hail of bullets when the police attacked his drug lab. He's dead. I'm here. I got thirty more years of my life than that stupid guy. I live in paradise. He's pushin' daisies."

Sandy was curious, "Do they all get their comeuppance?"

"Sooner or later," responded Peter. "But right away, you need to outwit them. But, that's not hard. I had to teach myself some moves. I read this book on martial arts, something about using his own weight to trip him up. Make him lunge at you and then step aside so he passes right through where you were. Let him fall of his own weight. I looked at every part of every move and figured it out. Letting evil pass right through you and out the other side. I practiced my moves and one day on the playground I pulled my trick and he went sprawling. All the other kids were so excited. His gang was scared. Kids were shaking my hand and some gave me their lunch money. I was a hero. I'd made the bully kid fall. Of course, he tried to beat the daylights out of me later on, but I made him fall, again. After that, he never bothered me again. "That's the secret, Sandy. You have to use the bully's own flaws to make his downfall. Figure out the bully's weakness and exploit it.

"You never fight on their ground. You never fight an army tank face on, you sneak around back and blow up the fuel trucks that feed the army tank. Find the weak link and attack there. Bully's don't think, Sandy, so in the long run, smart guys will win."

"You have to teach me those moves. I'd love to trip up Moe Lesko," said Sandy.

"Hey, my bully was named Moe too. Your Moe and my Moe— they are all scared down deep inside. Afraid of a bigger bully taking them down. They have to prove themselves by picking on you."

"Remember, Sandy"—Peter was on a rant—"you were reading the book. He ripped the pages out. You get smart. He stays stupid. It never works out for bullies.

"So, when we get back to the beach, I'll show you the moves to take down bullies. Meanwhile, we need to get back to digging," said Peter. Then he shook himself and said, "come on, let's see if we measured wrong."

There was a lot of pacing about and measuring.

"If you go halfway from these rocks to the tree, you land on Barney's spot, but if you go halfway from those rocks to the stump, you'd have a halfway point over here," said Peter as he paced off in a slightly different direction. "If we go from the edge of that stone to the edge of the stump and then try opposite edges the area that MIGHT be 'Half from tree to ruins' is still HUGE! Halfway from one big thing to another big thing is still big.

As they were both feeling exhausted and exasperated, there came a deafening noise from down the hill. A shrill high-pitched whistle and a clanking and thumping sound that made the ground shake. A huge machine coming in their direction.

"What is the heck is that?" asked Peter.

It was Ruth with Alice, the steam shovel, followed by Rhone in Ruth's jeep.

"I fixed it," Ruth yelled from the driver's seat. She jumped down and came over to Peter and Sandy, saying, "I've been fixing it whenever I had spare time for. After I heard Peter talking about that story with the kid and the steam shovel that could dig a whole basement in a day, I began to wonder if I could get Alice running. Turns out, there's a club of old guys online who keep old steam engines running. All it needed was a new inlet valve. I had to fix the cylinder oil tank, and the super-heater tubes need welding. The rest is ok. It's rusty but not a wreck."

"Yeah," said Rhone. "Rust runs faster here. Chaos comes quicker."

"Well, the rust is real," said Ruth, "but chaos doesn't defeat us when we beat it back and fix things. Alice runs great. Where do you want to dig?"

Peter pointed one way to where he thought they should dig, and Sandy pointed to another, while Nicky did a sit-and-paw at yet a different place.

"Ayuh Lawd," said Rhone. "Ah'yo' guys got no idea what you doin'. I'm getting some cold drinks whilst ah'yo' figure out wha'ch doin'"

"Maybe we should look at the map again," said Ruth.

They rolled out the leather scroll, and Sandy read again. "'Half from tree to ruins.' Then, there are those weird letters that look kind of like English but aren't any letters that I know. Wait, wait, wait! I saw this map in my dream, only on my map there were more of the funny letters across the bottom . . ."

"Come on, Sandy. You're dreaming stuff up," said Peter with disgust.

"No, wait a second," said Ruth. "So far, Sandy's dreams have given us good advice. We should see what's there.

With that, Sandy stretched out the scroll of leather and tried to make it as flat as he could. As he stretched the leather along the inner edge where it was tightly wound, there was a cracking sound as the ancient leather buckled and bent. Sandy bent the scroll sharply, and all kinds of dust and mold fell out of the creases and cracks in the leather. It looked like the leather had been home to insects who had carved tunnels in the leather, and as they brushed aside ages' worth of dust and mold, it became possible to make out letters, then whole words in the strange letters in that same weird alphabet.

"Aya looka wuk! What that is?" exclaimed a shocked and puzzled Rhone while coming back with the drinks. "None ah we saw that when de weird guy was showing us dat map. Wha's dere? Look at the strange squiggles dem."

ᛒᛏᚤᚤ ᚤᛁ ᛒᛉᚤᛍ ᚋᛁᛈ ᚤᛁᚋᛏ ᛏᛉᛍᛏᛏ ᚋᛁᚤᚋᛉᚱ ᛍᚋᚤᛍ

"This is no use," said Sandy as he stared at the lines.

"This is weird. What sense does this make? But it must be a clear message," said Ruth as she puzzled over the map. "Wait...no... unless...Hey, Peter, what was that line the pirates were yelling to you in your dream?"

"Oh. Oh, wait. Something about wanting bottles of rum. Boxes. Jugs. I don't remember."

"Good thing I wrote it down," said Ruth as she dug in a deep pocket for a notebook. "Hang on. I liked that line. Here it is, *'Pack my box with five dozen liquor jugs.'* What if Peter's dream pirate is telling us the code?"

"Look at this . . ." and her voice trailed off again. "Let's see how they line up. The word lengths are the same. Look at this. If you line up Peter's pirate line with this text on the map. Look, where there's an O in each English word there is this rune with two diagonal lines. Same with the I's. There are three I's and they all line up with these letters that look like I's. X lines up with two like a compound sound.

"Yes but the TH is just one of those "room" things. And X is using two."

"Well, that's the reality of runes. TH is one sound and X needs help from an S. but this is a code-breaker. We have a translation table, from runes to English. Peter dreamed up the line that matches this one on the map. Pretty stupid, these dreams, eh Peter?"

"What?" came Sandy's incredulous voice. "Rooms? That's like what the Vikings said. 'Rooms'. What are rooms?"

"Not rooms. It's *runes*," continued Ruth, Now that I'm seeing it all together, I can see this ancient alphabet. My father knew them. He taught me how to make them. We sent secret messages using the *runes* as our code. The map has a line of runes here at the bottom, and Peter's dream line is the code in English. No wonder that pirate was yelling at you."

"Wait, slow down," said Peter in an agitated voice. "These runes are hiding a message. And somehow on Water Island, a million miles from anywhere, and you know how to read them. How do you know that?"

"Oh, my poppa was a Norman," said Ruth. "His ancestors were from the Nordic countries. That's why his name is Norman. All 'Normans' know about runes. He just made sure that I knew. I wish I had seen this the first night. Now, we can figure out the message on the map. We have the translation table. We just have to decode it.

"De-code?" Sandy wasn't sure what that would entail.

"So let's look at the line of runes below the English that we've been reading. What does it say? The English is clear. "Half from tree to ruins."

And then this stuff—see how there are more letters in the lower line. It's different than the English.

ᚷᛏᛁᚹᚹᚱᛉᚤᛏᚱᛂᛏᛏᛉᚱᚢᛂᛏᛡᛏᛂᛏᛂ

Look," said Sandy. "I'll call out what it looks like and you find the English letter that stands for and write it down. So, they began with

Sandy calling out "It's like a straight up line with like arms up and legs down. Like a six-point star."

"That's H," said Ruth.

One bar with one diagonal going up."

"A," said Ruth.

"Straight bar with a right hook at the top."

"Um, just a sec, L," said Ruth.

And they continued in this manner, spelling out the message one letter at a time.

HALF FROM TREE TO RUNE STONE

"That sure is different," said Ruth as she peered over her notes.

"Must be a mistake," snapped Peter. "Runes instead of ruins. It's like a typo with a knife on leather.

"Or maybe it is runes," mused Ruth. "A rune stone. What rock up here could be called a 'rune stone'?"

"Rune stone. Tha's weird," said Rhone. "One ah dem boulder got lines cut in it. When we was small fry alla'we called dem Rhone stones. I thought dey was fo' me. We thought dey was from Taino native Americans. Never heard nothin' about no Vikings . . ."

"Oh, whoa, I forgot to tell you." Sandy said as his face lit up. "It must be that huge rock at the other end of the plain. One had lines on it. I saw them the night we were up here and found Barney's chest. I was so excited when Nicky barked and we found the chest that I never thought to tell you about the marks on that rock. Maybe they *are* runes. Maybe there's a message . . ."

"We need to translate the runes on that stone," cried Ruth.

"Well, leh we go," Rhone said over his shoulder as they all took off at a run to the large stones at the end of the plain.

There were several large boulders at that end of the plain. Sandy took a moment to remember which one had the lines but Rhone knew exactly which stone.

"He' ya go," said Rhone as he reached up to the lines in one boulder while Sandy climbed up to reach the grooves. "See how deh grooves is innna rock, ain' cracks but more like someone carve de rock. But a couple of dem but dey look like de runes on dat ledder scroll."

'Have at it with this wire brush," interjected Peter as he returned from Ruth's jeep with a bunch of tools—wire brushes, brooms, and the like.

"Be careful," Rhone had panic in his voice, "You don' wanna scrape and mash up de lines."

Sandy scraped dirt and moss out of the groves and began to reveal one rune after another.

We'll do it the way we did the other stuff," said Sandy. "I'll call out the lines, and you figure what it means and write it down.

ᚠᚢᛚᛚ ᛘᛜᛜᛏ ᛋᛖᛏ

"Straight up with two swirls to the right," said Sandy.

Ruth lined her finger with a character like that and called out, "that's an F."

"Yeah," said Sandy, "it kinda looks like an F."

The next one looks like a lowercase N."

That's U," said Ruth as they slowly worked out each letter. With a few errors and corrections, they spelled it all out:

FULL MOON SET

"That's better," said Ruth with a smug nod. "'Full Moon Set. I wonder why that . . .?"

"Well that is crazy," said Peter.

"Yeah," added Rhone. "No help a't'all."

Peter agreed, "It's not like it says go dig over there."

"Ah gentlemen, you're wrong," said Ruth. "We now know that this *is* the *rune stone*. If Vikings put them here, they weren't thinking about pirates. Those pirates didn't get here for hundreds of years. No, this is more like North'man graffiti, like a gang of boys vandalizing this place. They don't have spray paint in that era, so they carved this rock. So this stone is what the pirates used when they said, 'Half from tree to rune stone.' "

"Well that would take us to a very different place than where Nicky dug," said Peter.

"And all'a Barney's holes too," added Rhone, "Dis the odda side of de hilltop.

"Ok, ok, so Rhone you stand there," said Peter. "I'll take the string"

There was a lot of pacing off lines and directions. Ruth got out her long measuring tape and surveyor's gear. They were measuring here to there and back. Where is halfway? Which side of the stump are we using? Which side of the stone?"

"Wait a sec, fellas," Ruth said. "We don't need to know exactly where to dig. Alice can take this whole hilltop apart tonight."

Ruth had kept a good head of steam on Alice and she swung the shovel around, facing the hilltop and the huge treads clambered over everything in the way until Alice was sitting right where they planned to start digging.

"Wow," exclaimed Sandy, "That machine can go anywhere"

The steam shovel made short work of the place they picked. Within a few shovels full, Alice hit something that wasn't rocks or dirt.

"STOP, Ruth," yelled Peter. "That's the corner of something. I'll go at it by hand." Peter and Rhone dove into the trench with their shovels and began digging around the emerging chest.

While Peter was digging, Ruth rigged the flood lights on the extensible poles from her jeep, so there was bright light where they were working.

Out of the hole, Peter pulled a box. It was an old box with rusty hinges and a rusty latch that crumbled into dust as Peter tried to force it open. The box lid popped open, revealing a lot of . . . moldy old books.

"Jezum bread. Aya looka wuk. Nothin' but fusty, moldy books," exclaimed a very disappointed Rhone.

"Whoa, it may be moldy books, but we just proved to ourselves that there's more up here than Barney's one box," said Ruth, gleeful with the discovery of the second chest.

Finding a second treasure chest turned them from casual disbelievers into frenzied maniacs.

"Piper said two," said Peter.

"Yes," said Sandy, "but the pirates said twenty or more."

A few hours later, they hit a box with a few hundred silver coins. That's when the frenzy kicked up to high pitch.

They worked at a frantic pace into the night under Ruth's battery-powered extensible light. When Ruth's batteries ran out, they continued with flashlights. When the flashlights died, they continued with emergency flares and when they ran out of those, they continued in just the moonlight. They worked at each spot until they hit solid rock. In some places, the dirt layer was ten feet deep and in other spots, it was less.

In the wee hours, they hit big. At a spot about a quarter of the way from the tree stump to the rune stone was a huge deposit of chests. A dozen at one level and another dozen below them.

There were large boxes with iron locks, antique jewelry boxes, and leaden chests, strong boxes made of oak with iron bands, and chests with arched tops and leather straps that had rotted away ages ago.

One or two boxes were loaded with moldy old books and papers, but most were loaded with loot—real loot—the real thing. There were fancy jewelry boxes crammed with brooches and rings, all set with precious stones. There were small chests, the size of a breadbox, with a trove of gold dust, gold nuggets, and gold doubloons. One even had a hammered gold mirror. There were blocks of jade with ancient faces carved in the stone and all kinds of jewelry with emeralds and rubies. And there was box after box after box of silver escudos—pieces of eight . . . tens of thousands of silver coins.

They worked in the moonlight until they had dug up the whole plain. They dug at every spot until they hit solid rock and then moved on to the next spot. When they had disrupted the entire top of the hill and gotten to solid rock everywhere, they stopped.

They loaded all the chests into the jeeps, and then they all collapsed on a big, flat rock by the edge of the plain looking at the mountain top they had demolished.

"This is amazing," said an exhausted Peter. "We made a mess of this mountain, but we must have thousands of silver coins in all those chests. It's like five hundred pounds of silver."

"And there must be a few hundred pounds of gold too," added Ruth.

"Aya Lawd, da badd," said Rhone, "Dat's a pretty big fort-tune."

"What did we load, like 30 chests of loot?" mused Ruth. It *is* a fortune, Peter. And it's a good thing we hit bottom. Those pirates couldn't have dug down to solid rock like Alice did. Now we know we got it all." As she spoke, she looked around at the way they had turned over the entire top of the mountain.

Peter said, "Ruth, tell me how you fixed Alice again."

Ruth laughs, "I met these guys in an online discussion group who fix old steam engines. They helped with the parts. Then it was just about fixing and doing some welding."

"But why? Why'd you bother?" asked Peter quizzically.

"Because you told us that kid story from your dream, remember? I wanted to see if you would notice me if I made your dream come true. I hadn't imagined we'd dig for treasure."

"Is there anything you don't know, Ruth?" asked Peter.

"Sure Peter—how to get you to notice me," she shot back.

"Well, I notice you, now," said Peter. "You are pretty amazing. You're pretty, too. I don't think I ever saw your hair blow in the wind like this before . . ." Peter mused as he trailed off.

The four of them sat, exhausted, on the edge of the plain, looking over their dig site and catching the first hint of a dull indigo light in the east.

"Any cold soda left? "asked Ruth.

"Ah no. All'a ice done melt. All's we got is warm drinks. An' it's almost coffee time."

Peter had that vacant look he got when he was lost in thought. He was musing about Ruth. *She's utterly amazing*, he thought. *She's always been here, and she fixes everything, and she knows everything.*

"Hey Sandy," asked Peter in a light and vacant voice, "Do you suppose that Piper in my dream had a heart all lit up on the second jewelry chest like she's telling me it's ok to have a second love in my heart?"

"Well, you *are* your own dream dictionary, Peter. At least that's what they say in Knight School. Your images are from your life—like Piper with a second jewelry chest."

"What about you, Ruth? Could a dream tell me to open my chest to allow a new love into my heart?"

"Maybe," she said as she leaned over and put her head on his shoulder. "Maybe."

Rhone chuckled, "Jezum Bread, Peter, you soundin' like Sandy."

"Well, we *are* sitting on a small fortune because Sandy listened to his dreams," said Peter. "And I think I've found a new love by listening to my dream. Real treasure is in your heart."

"Oh, Peter, you such a romantic," interjected Rhone who then asked, "Bein' practical for a moment, are we gonna split this four ways? Even steven?"

"Yes, exactly. We four. Now Sandy has enough to save for college. I can pay off the bills that piled up. No. Wait! I can pay off the mortgage. We can just own Sandells without a worry. I can stay. And Ruth, ah, would you like to set up a, you know, like, a two-person . . . ya know . . . will you stay here with me? We could kinda live here together kinda forever."

She didn't raise her head from his shoulder as she made a soft, lingering, umming sound. Peter continued, "And Rhone, you have enough to . . ." Peter trailed off as he thought of Rhone being so rich that he never came back to the island.

"No Peter, don' worry. Rich or not, I ain' closin' Rhone's Reef and Sand Bar. Ahyo ain' movin' an; I standin' here wit you. I'll keep it open. I like the people dem."

Just then, Nicky came up to Sandy and sat and held out his paw. He had a stick in his mouth. Sandy did a quick check. Yes, it was an ordinary stick.

"What about Nicky? Is he getting a share? After all, he found the chest," said Sandy.

"Whoa—he found an empty chest. But he did know where to look. It's like that dog is clairvoyant," said Peter, "Sure, Nicky gets all the hot dogs he wants for the rest of his life."

"Just hot dogs?"

"Oh, ok, we'll get him chopped liver too. Whatever he wants."

"What about Elroy?" asked Sandy.

"Well, he's off-island at Saint Fritzister's Day," said Rhone. He's deh Gran' Marshall."

"Oh, ok," sighed Peter. "We'll do something for Elroy too, even if he's never around when I need him. Maybe he gets the moldy books." And they all laughed.

"ok," Rhone said, "just so in yo' heart yo' takin' care of evvy one."

That's when Ruth wondered aloud, "We found the Rune stone. Why do you suppose that rune stone say 'Full Moon Set"?

Sandy sat bolt upright, "Hey, that's right now. We've been digging all night, under a full moon. We are about to see the moon set."

With that, they all turned away from the flat plain they had just dug up and turned to look west as the full moon was just above the horizon.

Sandy said, "At Knight School, they say this is dream time, the wee hours of morning. This is the time of night when dreams happen. And we're here to see it . . ."

As he trailed off, the full moon began to kiss the horizon, slipping into the ocean. "It's as pretty as sunset but with blue light," he continued as the sparkling moonlight reached across the ocean right into his eyes. Behind him, in the east, the sun was getting ready to rise, lighting the east with pale light. Two lights. One rising and one setting. "This is the moment of new beginnings," Sandy muttered.

Peter had his arm around Ruth, and she had hers around him. Her head was still resting on his shoulder.

"I know what we're beginning," said Peter as he held Ruth closer.

Sandy said, "And I'm beginning to understand that you can't love anyone if you don't love yourself. I had to keep loving me even when you and the pirates and all were laughing at me."

"Whoa Mehson," said Rhone with a low whistle. "Now you soundin' like Auntie. You gotta find love in your heart for yourself.' That's wha' Auntie used'ta say."

Sandy had his arm around Nicky, and Rhone was on the other side of Nicky as they watched the moon setting into the ocean.

Peter turned to Sandy and said, "ok, so maybe your dream stuff isn't all crazy. What is this Knight School you go to . . .?"

12

Epilogue

"Stand down, you scurvy scallywag! Lay down yer sword and swear allegiance to me pirate band, and ye live—or keep yer sword and spar with Captain Feit. I give no quarter."

Sandy felt the heat of the big man's breath on his face, the barrel chest, the long arm, huge with muscle, his fist holding a sharp cutlass. The other arm had a hook. The pirate band, gnarly men, held their swords high, chanting a bloodthirsty rhyme.

Sandy held firm, head up, and yelled, "No! I am not walking the plank, and I am not going to let you make me do anything. You're being a bully. You're just a puffed-up big bully with a scared child inside you. I am not going to let you do that to me anymore." Sandy raised himself up to his full height. He stood with his shoulders squared in the power posture and did not flinch."

The pirates were stunned. Their song and chant stopped. Feit dropped his sword in stunned silence, then recovered and lurched as if to grab Sandy. Nicky was at the ready, snarled, and grabbed Feit's arm in powerful jaws. The burly man leapt back calling to his crew, "Sic 'em men. Get the kid."

"No. Not this time Captain Feit. I'm not backing down," said a defiant Sandy.

"He's right, Captain Feit," came the voice of Peter Sandell, who had suddenly emerged and stood by Sandy's side. Peter had neither swords nor pistols but modern guns, grenades, and explosives. And behind Peter was a whole army of soldiers and their gear.

The three in front—Sandy, Peter, and Nicky—stood firm and united as Feit and the pirates backed off.

"Looks like you brought a knife to a gunfight, Captain Feit. You're outgunned," said Peter.

"And out-dogged too," added Sandy.

"Woof" added Nicky as he sat and raised his paw.

"No one ever stood up to me before," said Captain Feit with tears welling up in his eyes. Trembling, he fell to his knees and started to cry. "Being a tough guy isn't working for us anymore," He blubbered and all the pirates collapsed . . .

Sandy touched Nicky's paw, and they took off, leaving Peter to tend to the defeated pirates.

Sandy was flying. High in the clouds, skimming the tops of the clouds, diving into the mist and up and out again, side by side with Nicky. Hand touching paw. They were flying to . . . To? To where?

"Let's find those Vikings. We can help them fix their long ship. Ruth found plans on a website. I saw it. I memorized the parts that would help Rundwulf and Whorf get their ship back in order.

"Hey, I came back."

"Look Rundwulf, shouted Whorf. "The new world boy is back."

"Yo, Sandy. Thou came back to see oss," said Whorf.

"I brought you something. I dug deeper like you said and I found the plans you need to fix the langskip." With that, Sandy rolled out a scroll with all the instructions to make repairs. "And I brought tools," he added, opening a bag of tools that Ruth had given him.

"She said this is a gift from her heart to the Northmen . . . So, you can go back."

"Oh, no, no, vee never go back. Vee are the leading edge. When vee fix ship, Vee go on. What is over the next horizon? If not for this Viking spirit, vee humans would all still be back in the old country . . ."

As Whorf spoke, the gang of men all sang out as one,

"Ever Onward
That's our spirit!
Ever Onward,
Never quit."

With that, Sandy reached out to Nicky and touched the dog's paw, and immediately, they were up in the clouds on their way to Knight School, leaving the Viking ship to glide out into the full moon set.

"Ok, everyone, enough of this masquerade," said Reed. "Sandy got to the end of the story. It's time to reveal ourselves."

Blake stepped up for a bow and said, "I played Captain Feit and Rundwulf. I'm such a swashbuckling pirate, arrrrr."

Grace bowed and said, "I played Bonny Anne. Women rock. Fierce, smart, and bold. Women make men; men don't make anything."

"And I played Whorf," said Kat, "another powerful and knowledgeable woman. With powerful ideas about language and consciousness. I really like her."

"Mars played Porklington," said Blake with a laugh.

"Norman Porklington that is," said Mars. "That pirate was smart and wily. He had some Nordic roots and knew about the runes and pretended to work for Captain Feit while he was figuring out how to stash the loot. He was the only one who knew everything. When the pirates were captured, he made out to be the cook and got away without being hung. He had the map stashed away. That's how it got to Elmer Barney. Good man; wily, though."

"Reed," came the voice of Grace. "Can we bring other people to Knight School?"

"You already have."

☾ ✪ ☽

Back in *WakeWorld*, Sandy had enough money for college. Peter and Ruth settled into life at Sandell's . . . with no renters. Rhone buried his treasure and made a map.

Peter was puzzled that Rhone buried his share. And asked, "Why'd you bury your share of the treasure?"

"Time Langa dan Twine," responded Rhone as he was wiping down the counter of his bar.

"Wait, I know, another of Aunties sayings. What does that one mean?"

"You don' know? Man, ayou folks ain' know shit.

Auntie used ta say that all'a time."

"As far as I can tell, Rhone," said Peter, "Auntie was saying something *all the time*." Now, you're saying her stuff."

"Cause it all true. Time longa dan twine. Them boxes of coins and stuff—they been in the ground for all dem ages. Now, I got it, and what I gonna do, sell the coins, dem? No. I gon' leave them buried. I always know if I need 'em that I got 'em. Tha's real. Gotta go with real."

"So what's auntie's old saying mean?"

"'Time langa dan twine?' Wisdom of age prevails over all things."

"So why didn't you say *that*?"

"Like Sandy said, 'When you use dey words, they come alive in you.' So I's talkin' wit Auntie all de time."

And it turns out that the moldy books they gave to Elroy were actually rare volumes that took the auction world by storm, and Elroy ended up with more loot than all of them . . .

Afterword

A note to the reader. This is a work of fiction. There is a real Water Island in the *WakeWorld*. But ours is not that island. None of the people are real, though some may resemble people I have known or share people's names. None of this is real—except the story of buried treasure on Water Island.

I took a lot of liberties with the pirates and Vikings. I apologize to any serious student of Old Norse or Runes that I have translated some runes into English and some into Old Norse. Please forgive me. On the other hand, I hope you find them delightful, look for the messages in runes in the art, and use the runes to create your own secret messages. A special thanks to www.valhyr.com. I used their rune converter. All errors are my own.

Many thanks to my dream teacher, Henry Reed. He is the man most responsible for the modern interest in the dreaming mind. He read the draft, and I'm grateful for his comments. He was the professor at my Knight School.

Big thank you to Fred Ridder and Pamela Wesson who are dear friends from Princeton. They did persnickety reading of punctuation to told me everything that was wrong. It was like a semicolonoscopy. Thank you, Fred. Thank you Pam.

A special thank you to Dr. Chinzera Davis-Kahina of the Caribbean Cultural Center of the University of the Virgin Island and Dr. Gillian Royes from UVI. They reviewed Rhone's eastern Caribbean creole for accuracy and approved Auntie's idiomatic phrases. After twenty-five years living in the islands, I wanted Rhone to sound like my friends.

I am delighted to work with Candace Lovely. We have been friends for decades, and I simply adore her work. I love you, Candace. Go buy a painting from Candace at www.candacelovely.com.

I am deeply grateful to April Knight who researched and developed the rune art for the chapter titles. She caught me in the present tense and forced me back into the past.

A special warm thought for Dr. Margaret Mead. She led me to study dream practices in remote cultures.

Special thanks to all the parents and children in the Princeton ParentNet who read my stories to their kids.

This book started when I discovered that my family name came to England with the Norman invasion. Randall comes from Randolf, and Randwolf came from Rundwulf. The NorthFolk called their round shields a "Rund," and the Wolf is obvious. So, the Randall's are *Shield Wolf* people.

The ideas in my books about dreams are entirely sound. You can solve problems in dreams. You can help each other by giving your dreams to someone in need. You can communicate by dreaming. Ask your family members about their dreams and discuss them.

You do it every night. Pay attention.

Pack my box with five dozen liquor jugs

ᛒᛅᚴᚴ ᛘᛁ ᛒᚬᚴᛋ ᚢᛁᚦ ᚠᛁᚢᛅ ᛏᚬᛋᛅᚾ ᛚᛁᚴᚢᚬᚱ ᛋᚢᚴᛋ

Alexander Randall 5th is the author of three Dream Wizard books. He has been a professor at the University of the Virgin Islands. Among other subjects, he teaches the Psychology of Sleep and Dreaming and classes in Creative Problem Solving.

An as entrepreneur, he created the Boston Computer Exchange – the world's first e-commerce business and later he created the East West Education Foundation which recycled computers and supported democracy around the world in the 1980's as the Soviet Union was falling.

Randall is the author of "Dream Wizard Conquers his Knight Mare" and "Dream Wizard ESCAPES" among many publications.

He took his doctoral degree at Columbia University under the direction of Dr. Margaret Mead working on the origins of novel ideas. His dissertation arose from a field study among a tribe of dreamers. He holds various Master's degrees from Columbia. He has a bachelor's degree in Psychology from Princeton where he studied sleep and dreaming with Dr. Henry Reed. His research involves the psychology of the visionary experience, creativity, innovation, entrepreneurship and the edges of insanity.

His web sites include:

www.dream-wizard.com
www.alexrandall5.com
www.alex5.com
www.dr-dream.com
www.outskirtspress.com/life-lessons
en.wikipedia.org/wiki/Boston_Computer_Exchange

CZ ✪ ℘

Who Is Candace Whittemore Lovely?

With a fussy child on her hands, Mrs. Sally Lovely gave her daughter Candace a red crayon to calm and entertain her. That one act started a life time of imagination and creation for Candace Whittemore Lovely.

Her passion for art has continued to flourish and shape her life choices. In high school she led a strike to keep the art room open. She would skip study hall to go home and create in her dad's workshop. An art major in college, she was awed by Winslow Homer's works. She asked one professor, "who can teach me to paint like him?" He replied, "NO ONE!"

That didn't stop Candace. After graduating with a bachelor's degree in art and a fifth-year teaching certificate, she moved to Boston. Her husband took her to the best art Gallery on Newbury Street. There Bill Vose recommended Candace study with the Boston School, America's oldest continuing school of painting. The Boston School developed her under a philosophy based on impressionistic observation of light and color. Candace eventually owned a Fenway Studio where John Singer Sargent once painted. Her career has flourished as she has earned awards and Hall of Fame honors.

In 1991 Lovely painted the official portrait of Barbara Bush in the First Lady's Garden at the White House. She is a University of Vermont Most Prominent Alumna and a Copley Society Master. Candace has been referred to as "the top American living female impressionist artist" and "The Grand Dame of Boston Painters". Sold throughout the world, many of her works have depicted life and landscapes from New England and the Low Country. Her paintings capture the moment. Whether it's a polo match, an old man shucking peas, umbrellas at the beach, or a Vermont pasture, her work embraces the scene and use light and color to express life and love.

Her web sites:

https://www.candacelovely.com/
https://candace-lovely.pixels.com/collections/water+island

CPSIA information can be obtained
at www.ICGtesting.com
Printed in the USA
BVHW011418250822
645339BV00007B/10